The Dom Tames Rapunzel

by

Sydney St. Claire

Once Upon a Dom Book Five

The Dom Tames Rapunzel

Contact Information: info@thewildrosepress.com

Cover Art by *Diana Carlile*

The Wild Rose Press, Inc.
PO Box 708
Adams Basin, NY 14410-0708

Visit us at www.thewilderroses.com

Publishing History
First Scarlet Rose Edition, 2016
Print ISBN 978-1-5092-0984-2
Digital ISBN 978-1-5092-0972-9

Published in the United States of America

In high school, they were adversaries. Now, he's her Dom. Can she submit?

"I guess you don't recognize me. It has been many years." He forced disappointment into his voice.

Jessica whipped around, head high as she glared down the gentle slope of her nose at him. "I know who you are. *Sir*."

Her acknowledgment pleased him, as did the spark of resentment rolling off her in waves. "Ah, a sub with spunk."

Jasen admitted to a bit of perverse pleasure that she was required to show deference to his Dom status, and the fact that it didn't sit well with her made him wonder whether she was truly submissive. Or was her reluctance because he'd been the nerd from high school, the one person who didn't bow to her bidding.

Of course, it was more likely this was just another game in a long list of games, parties, and wasting her life on the frivolous. "We've determined we're not strangers, so back to my question. Will you accept my invitation to be my sub for the fairy tale event? I need your answer. Now." He deepened his voice, used his most commanding tone.

Jessica swallowed hard in reaction and quickly lowered her eyes, but not before he caught a hint of pure lust. His interest rose even higher. Perhaps Glorie was right in her assessment of this woman from his past. Still, she wasn't like the rest of the subs who adhered to their places and roles. If she agreed to be his sub, he accepted that he was going to have to tame this princess. He looked forward to the challenge.

Dedication

To All My Readers. Wishing you all the best.
Take the time each day to find joy, whether it is a hug
and kiss from a loved one, or a beautiful flower in a
garden or the song of a bird.

Chapter One

Sitting in his club, Jasen McPherson was about to make the biggest mistake of his life, he who was cautious, careful and controlled.

"I'm game," he told the Domme across from him. "Add me to your guest list."

He'd heard there was another BDSM event being planned at Pleasure Manor. Their events were legendary. He'd taken part in many, but so far, had not attended any of the famed fairy tale themed events.

"Do you have a sub in mind?"

Loud cheers and applause from across the room nearly drowned Glorie Amadori's question. The demo on spanking had ended.

His gaze shifted to a tall, blonde wearing a skimpy red dress that revealed more than concealed. *Don't do it. Don't be a fucking fool. You will regret it. Do. Not. Go. There.*

But did he listen to his own advice? Of course not. He jerked his head toward his choice. "Jessica Lowe." The moment he spoke the subs name, his gut clenched, and his cock jumped to attention. *Yep, big mistake.*

Sharing his table at the popular BDSM club, Top to Bottom, Glorie speared him with an incredulous stare. "You can't be serious. You want to sponsor the clubs spoiled princess?"

He shrugged, his gaze on the woman seated on a leather couch with several other subs waiting for Doms without partners to choose them for an evening of fun and games. A Dom approach her, but she refused, and the Dom strode away. "Why the hell not?"

Glorie leaned back in her chair, regarded him thoughtfully as she tapped her red-tipped nails on the table. "Why not, indeed? I've never seen you with her, nor have I heard of you choosing her for your evening entertainment."

"I haven't." Thinking back to high school and the school's rich, spoiled little darling, he smiled grimly. "But I know her."

The Domme knew the value of silence. As did Jasen. He waited her out.

She motioned to a sub serving water or soft drinks to the exclusive clientele and held up her empty water bottle, then inclined her head. "You're good, Master McPherson."

He grinned and stretched out his feet, his gaze sweeping the lounge and everyone wandering through on their way into the play area. He eyed two identical Doms. Both wore leather vests and not much else. The twins were in the house. Some sub would be happy. "As are you, Mistress. Is there a problem with my choice? After all, you asked."

Glorie's dark eyes sparked with interest and speculation. She laughed low in her throat. "Not at all. You simply caught me off guard. You know as well as I that Jessica is a rather troublesome sub."

"Now that is an understatement, Mistress.

She's only been coming here for what—three weeks? The woman's a master at manipulation. She's got the Doms in an uproar as they end up doing *her* bidding."

Chuckling, Glorie broke open her water and took a sip. "It will take a strong Dom to control her. New and inexperienced Dom's don't stand a chance."

"Good thing I'm not new or inexperienced. I do admit to being surprised she's submissive. I know how much she likes to give orders." Yeah, that too was an understatement, for he knew firsthand how difficult, demanding, and spoiled she was.

"Then you also know when it comes to sex, many who wield power day to day prefer a more submissive role in one area of their life." Glorie eyed a submissive male who'd just entered the large lounge.

Seeing her interest, he chuckled softly. "But not you, Mistress."

She laughed, pulled out a short riding crop from the belt around her waist, and bent it into an arch, her features thoughtful. "No, not me. I prefer being in charge of all aspects of my life. But Jessica truly is submissive. She's a very troubled young woman, I think. Not at all happy."

"Poor little rich girl. She can have whatever she wants, whomever she wants. What a sad life."

The Domme smacked the back of his hand with her riding crop. "We each have our crosses to bear. Money isn't everything. Now, back to your invite. Is this to be a revealed invitation or do you prefer your identity kept secret?"

Most events at Pleasure Manor were masked affairs to protect identities as the private and very exclusive club membership included rich and powerful men and women. Some preferred to keep their lifestyle preferences private for personal reasons, others in deference to their careers.

"Revealed." He could just imagine Jessica's reaction to an invitation to participate in the upcoming Fairy Tale event as his sub. *If* she even remembered him. High school was a good ten years ago.

Back then, she didn't *hang* with the in crowd, she'd *ruled* that crowd of ass kissers and worn her homecoming crown as though she had royal blood. She'd floated through school, batting her long lashes and manipulating others to do her work for her.

Teachers and staff feared her father, boys ran to do her bidding in the hopes of dating or fucking her, and girls she'd handpicked to be her entourage did whatever she wanted in order to stay in her good graces and receive coveted invites to parties at her family's mansion. And him?

He'd been a nerd, captain of the debate team, into computers and gaming, and not even a speck on her radar. He didn't go to parties, dances, or the school sports events. He'd been invisible and too busy working hard to earn a scholarship to be the first in his family to go to college.

And she'd nearly ruined his perfect 4.0 GPA. More concerned with her looks than homework and reports, she'd assumed he'd do all the work when they were lab partners for their entire senior year.

The spoiled little rich girl had been wrong. From what he'd seen and read in the news or in social media, not much had changed. She still partied, had her flock of girlfriends, and skated through life with everyone else doing for her what she should be doing for herself.

"How about Rapunzel for her fairy tale character?" Glorie sent him a wicked look. "Rapunzel gets her Dom instead of her prince." She had a pen in hand and an invitation on the table.

"Rapunzel? Princess in a tower with long, blonde hair?" At Glorie's nod, he grimaced. That certainly fit Jessica as her hair when not worn in a fancy braid around her head was well past her ass. "Yeah, that works. High up in her tower where she can lord it over everyone. And if you're going to synop this, it should be The Dom Tames Rapunzel." He had a feeling he had his work cut out for him.

Glorie narrowed her eyes and firmed her lips. "Just remember, in the fairy tale, Rapunzel was put there by a parent who was overprotective, caging her and keeping her from growing and experiencing life. There are all kinds of prisons, Master McPherson." She penned the character's name onto the invite.

Jasen grimaced. "Your degree is showing, Mistress. I think you're a bit off. Jessica Lowe experiences her world very well. Jet-setting here and there, shopping, parties, and attending one gala or event after another."

"Yes, she's a bit of a social butterfly—"

"An understatement, Mistress." A bark of laughter escaped.

Jessica had money, and she flaunted it. She was everything he disliked from her poor, rich girl lifestyle to her father who cared little for the environment or the innocent people who stood in his way of making a few more bucks to add to his vast fortune. And to Jessica's party allowance. No, he had no great love for the Lowe Empire so why was he even considering taking Princess Lowe on for a three-day event?

Glorie straightened and sent him what he thought of as her scary-Domme face. "You listen to me, Jasen. I don't know your connection to her, though I can guess the issues you'd have with her father, but she is not responsible for what that man does or doesn't do. She's an unhappy woman who has everything, yet she has nothing."

He held up his hands in surrender. "Okay, got it. She can't help being a spoiled, rich girl."

"You'd best behave, Master McPherson." She studied him, eyes narrowed, lips firm. Then suddenly, she smiled, a rather wicked and nasty grin. "You just might be good for her. She could use a friend."

Well aware of the Domme's matchmaking tendencies, Jasen pointed a finger at her. "Don't even think about going there. Not interested in friendship. She wants fun. I'll give her fun. She's a big girl, Mistress. It's time for her to grow up." He narrowed his eyes when a Dom in cheap fake leather, studs, and latex approached Jessica. "Speaking of new and inexperienced."

"Come with me, sub."

The Dom's loud demand had Glorie whipping

around in her seat. "Oh dear."

Jasen didn't catch Jessica's reply but saw her shake her head no.

"Do what you're told, slave." The clueless Dom reached down and yanked Jessica to her feet. "I'm in charge."

Jasen winced and then sighed. This time, he didn't blame Jessica for refusing the wannabe. "Our door monitors are slipping, Mistress." Tops and Bottoms was an exclusive club and not open to everyone who fancied trying out the BDSM lifestyle. Every Dom had to be vouched for and vetted, had to prove he or she had training and knew what they were doing. Subs were given more leeway but still had to be approved before they could participate in any activity.

Glorie half rose.

"Relax, Mistress. She can handle herself. That poor sap is going to be cut off at the knees." He'd seen Jessica in action many times since she joined the club. Sure enough, the woman straightened, head up, shoulders back, and glared at the man like a regal queen ready to cut her minion to shreds with words alone.

He was too far to hear her words, but when the Dom refused to release her, she followed through on his next tug, sending her fist into the man's soft belly, then stomping her heel onto the man's instep. The man yelled and stumbled back.

At that point, Jasen nodded to one of the clubs orange-vested DM's waiting for his signal. The DM, who was a small mountain, whipped the Dom's hands behind his back and perp-walked the man out.

"I'll find out who let him in." Glories' voice was low and tight. She stood, tall and sleek in her scary Domme attire of black bustier, short, leather skirt that barely hid her crotch, fishnet stockings, and pencil thin heels. She nodded. "Call Hastings to set up an appointment so we can plan your weekend. There'll also be a meeting of Doms to go over the weekend's planned activities. Not required, but as you're not hiding your identity, I expect to see you there."

Jasen nodded. Glorie, an imposing figure in five-inch heels, strode toward another DM, spoke briefly, and then headed to Jessica Lowe. Once again, his attention focused on the blonde bombshell. What the hell was he thinking? He had a big charity event to pull together and didn't have the time or energy for spoiled rich girls or an encounter that was sure to stir his emotions—and not for the better.

He pulled out his phone, flipped it to his photo app, and thumbed through until he found an old picture of Jessica Lowe that his photographer buddy had taken at a football game. She was staring into the camera, yet not seeing, her eyes unfocused. A strand of her silky, wind-blown hair curled around her jaw and lower mouth like a lover's hand.

She was so damn beautiful. Hauntingly so. But what struck him every time he glanced at the photo was how sad and lonely she appeared—a lost, little girl on the verge of tears. He stared into her electric-blue eyes and felt himself sinking, caught between the devil and the deep, blue sky.

"Yep, making a big mistake, buddy." He was that train wreck waiting to happen, yet he couldn't stop himself from hurtling toward disaster.

****

Jessica Lowe was bored. Two Doms had approached, and she'd declined both. She'd served each before and wasn't in the mood for either. No spark, no excitement. Just sex. Nothing outstanding in her mind, and not worth working up the sweat for. The third Dom had been a jerk. Imagine, thinking he could order her about as though she had no choice.

She sat back in her cushioned seat and scanned the bar, picking out several male subs at one end, and a lone Domme chatting with the bartender at the other. The DM who'd escorted the jerk out returned and took up his position just inside the lounge. Couples of both sexes and various combinations occupied each small, round topped table. The room hummed with low laughter, conversation, and no action. The two female subs who'd joined her had gone off to explore the offerings of the club, leaving her to sit by herself.

She sighed. "Time to leave."

San Francisco's nightlife was legendary. There was always a party somewhere and her name got her in wherever she wanted. The appeal of surrounding herself with loud, throbbing music, the energy that came from a crowd dancing and flirting, and a ton of noise and action sounded better than just sitting like a lump on a couch. She wrinkled her nose at her untouched glass of diet soda. She definitely needed a drink.

Like most BDSM clubs, Tops and Bottoms didn't serve alcohol. She uncrossed her legs. Time to blow this boring place, find a real party where she'd drink too much, and dance until she was exhausted. Then sleep most of tomorrow away.

And wake bored, looking for another venue to let off steam. God, she was pathetic. Maybe she should go to Paris for a couple weeks. Except Paris wouldn't be any different from San Francisco. Same parties, same clubs, same boring people.

Her restless gaze swept the lounge and returned to the wet-my-panties Handsome Hunk. Talk about some sweet eye candy. Too bad, he was way over there and she was here, all by her lonesome. Of course, the fact that he was sitting with Glorie Amadori, one of the club owners, and a Domme herself, meant that HH was probably Glorie's sub for the evening. Yeah, a real shame as she wouldn't mind trying that yummy male out.

To her surprise, Glorie stood, spoke briefly to the DM, then headed her way. Jessica lowered her gaze respectfully. The Domme was a powerful woman, one who commanded respect. She wasn't as rich as Jessica but certainly more powerful, both in the BDSM world and out.

Jessica clasped her hands together. God, was Glorie looking for a female sub tonight? The idea didn't repulse Jessica. She'd taken part in threesome's before, but the other females were always subs. She got hot and tingly just thinking about being submissive to the Queen of Dommes. Glorie was legendary in her demands and the pleasure she meted out.

"Look at me, sub."

Jessica met Glorie's dark gaze. "How may I serve you, Mistress?"

Glorie lifted a finely arched brow. "Would you serve me, Jessica?"

Gnawing her lower lip, she pressed her hands into her belly to stop the nervous flutters. It'd been one thing to be a part of a threesome where her attention, and that of the other sub, was on the Dom and his needs. She'd never been with a woman one on one or been fucked by a woman.

"I don't know, Mistress," she answered honestly. God, the thought turned her on, yet scared her at the same time. She could imagine being spanked by the Domme, had seen her give a few demonstrations, but wasn't sure she was brave enough to engage sexually.

Glorie laughed softly. "That's very honest of you, sub. Rest assured, I'm not asking that of you. Tonight."

The wicked gleam in her eyes warned Jessica that the Domme thought the idea had merit. Her heart pounded, and a bead of sweat ran down her spine.

"Yes, Mistress," she murmured respectfully even as the very thought of serving Glorie bounced like a tiny ball in her mind, ping ponging wildly from fear to lust. Good heavens. She quickly lowered her gaze so she didn't have to see the speculation growing in those dark, dark eyes.

The woman laughed low in her throat. "Not so brave tonight, are you, little sub." She held out an envelope.

Taking it, Jessica saw her name penned in fancy calligraphy. "What's this?"

"Open it." Glorie leaned down, revealing cleavage ready to spill from her bustier, and the hint of dusky areolas. She raised Jessica's chin with a red-tipped nail. "One day, Jessica Lowe, I'll spank that lovely ass of yours and then I'll fuck you."

Jessie gulped as the Domme released her and strolled away on fuck-me icepick heels. *Holy shit.* In fact, a threesome with two Doms held a lot of appeal. *Damn*, she'd gone from bored and dry as a bone to excited and damp. She watched Glorie snap her fingers at a male sub kneeling on the carpet. He rose, allowed her to hook a leash to the collar around his neck. Glorie sent her one last wicked grin as she led her sub from the lounge.

To calm her suddenly, overactive system, she turned her attention to the envelope. A hum of excitement, like what came from opening a gift and finding what you wanted but hadn't dared to hope for sang through her body. The word in the clubs was Pleasure Manor was putting on another of their exclusive events. To date, she hadn't managed to snag an invitation. She'd learned the hard way that neither money, nor her daddy's name, could buy her way into that private and much sought after club membership.

Appreciating the weight and quality of the creamy envelope, she opened it and slid out a four by six card made from thick parchment paper that looked old and, from her experience, was penned on very expensive, hand-made stock. The lettering was also an old world script. A banner style logo stretched across the top. In the center, an embossed metallic blue castle gleamed with the words *The Kingdom of Dom* done in a fancy, swirly script beneath.

Her heart raced. She'd gotten one of the coveted invites. All feelings of being bored fled as she read.

You are hereby invited to Pleasure Manor for a weekend of pure pleasure. Event begins Thursday afternoon and ends Sunday after brunch.

Theme: Fairy Tales, The Stories Your Mother Never Read You.

Jessica nearly jumped up to do a boogie dance. She was going to Pleasure Manor for three delicious days of fun and wild sex. The rumors she'd heard about Pleasure Manor were enough to make a sub weep. She continued reading, noting the handwritten addition, Glorie's pen, no doubt, as she was usually the host.

Your Character: Rapunzel

Your Dom: Jasen McPherson.

Costumes provided. Formal ball Saturday evening. Instructions will be delivered.

Jessica blinked and reread the name of her sponsor. Jasen McPherson? She read it again and frowned. An image of a tall, skinny nerd with short black hair flitted through her mind.

Nah, it couldn't be the same boring, nerd from her senior year in high school. She grimaced. The boy she remembered had refused to do her share of the assignments and was probably the only guy in the entire student body who hadn't tried to date or bed her.

Not that she hadn't done her best to lure him in with sex so he'd do whatever she wanted. No guy had ever turned her down, but he'd treated her like a nasty, crawling bug and had taken delight in stomping her beneath his feet during that last year of school.

Good heavens. She hadn't thought of him since…since leaving school. She had to admit, his rejection had stung, as had the harsh words he'd flung at her each time she refused to do her share of a project. Even now, after—she ticked off the years—after nearly ten years, she remembered one fight after she'd tried her damnedest to seduce him.

He'd said she was the last girl he'd fuck, that she was nothing more than a spoiled rotten, greedy brat. And *he'd* had the gall to threaten to get a new partner if she didn't pull her weight.

She grimaced. Wearing her righteous indignation and fury as she often wore her furs to her father's parties, she'd gone to the teacher in tears to ask for a new partner, determined to show Jasen McPherson that she didn't need him. Plenty of others were more than willing to do her bidding.

Except there weren't any other students without partners, and the teacher refused to change partners around. Her choice had been to work it out with Jasen or do the class projects on her own. And that she couldn't do. At least Jasen gave her directions. Well, orders. He'd told her what to do, how to do it, and if it wasn't up to his standards, he made her do it again. She tapped the corner of the card on her thigh. Her last year of school had been hell, and it had been his fault.

Sliding the card back in the envelope, she considered. Maybe it wasn't such a surprise to discover he was a Dom. He'd certainly been bossy and demanding. And mean. Still considering the invite and staring at the envelope, she suddenly glanced around. Was he here in the club? Had he changed so much that she hadn't recognized him. Oh god, had she refused him?

A shiver of realization skittered from shoulders to knees. OMG. Her head slowly turned toward the table Glorie had vacated. The man she'd taken for the woman's sub seemed familiar, but she'd assumed she'd seen him in one of the clubs she favored. Studying him anew, recognition dawned. From skinny nerd to sexy Dom, there sat Jasen McPherson.

She recognized that square jaw, the dip in the chin that had always fascinated her. He'd lost the soft, roundedness of youth, and his features were sharp and distinct from cheeks to nose to jawline. He wore a white shirt that set off his deeply tanned features.

Her gaze drifted across his football field wide shoulders and temptingly hard, firm chest. She nearly swallowed her tongue. The pale nerd who'd been a pain in her ass was gone. *Unbelievable. It was really Jasen McPherson.*

As though he felt her eyes on him, Jasen shifted in his seat and met and held her gaze. For a long, heart-stuttering moment, she lost herself in bright green eyes that went so well with his black hair curling across the nape of his neck.

God, who knew the nerd would grow into one

hell of a sexy Dom. His mouth, those full, sensual lips curved with mocking amusement, jolting her out of her shocked amazement. Caught staring, she flushed, but damn, the invitation and the blast back into the past left her stunned. Hell, it left her speechless and wondering just how much he'd changed. He crooked his finger.

Her jaw dropped, and for a moment, she was back in high school with him bossing her around. Who did he think he was? Then she sighed. Oh yeah, he was a Dom. She didn't have to engage with him sexually, but she did have to show him proper respect.

Lowering her eyes, she sashayed to stand before him. "Yes, Sir? Do you wish me to serve you?"

Say yes. She was definitely intrigued and no longer bored. She wanted him to ask her to be his sub tonight. Then she'd decide if she wanted to accept the invitation to be his Dom for three days, though no one in his or her right mind would turn down the chance to take part in any event at Pleasure Manor.

"You received your invitation." His voice was deep, dark, like a mixture of rich chocolate and thick caramel sliding through her veins, leaving her dripping with a sweet gooey feeling from the tip of her head to her red-painted toes and everywhere in between, especially between her legs.

His gaze dipped to her breasts. Her nipples tightened, and her body hummed with desire. She bowed submissively even though it went against everything inside her to submit to his man. "Yes,

Sir. Thank you for the honor."

"Do you accept?"

Damn. She really wanted to try him out first. "I don't know, Sir. I don't know you."

Chapter Two

"We know each other, Miss Lowe." Jasen studied Jessica, allowed his gaze to roam over her face, studying each feature from her arched brows—a shade darker than her hair—long, thick lashes blackened, a faint smattering of freckles she tried to hide with makeup to her full, heart-shaped lips. Her smooth cheeks flushed with embarrassment—and did he dare hope—arousal?

She was taller than average but less than his own six-foot frame, and her body curved in all the right places. The low cut of her bodice revealed generous creamy swells, and her jutting nipples strained against the thin fabric. His gaze flicked from one to the other, inwardly pleased that they hardened further with just his look.

His dick stirred as waves of heat slid through his bloodstream like the ocean greedily swallowing as much land as it could reach. He glanced lower, finding no fault with her nipped in waist or the flare of her hips or— He swallowed. Some men went for tits, others for asses. He was a leg man, and Jessica had herself a pair of fucking hot legs, especially in her fuck-me heels. He didn't understand how women could walk on two five-inch nails, but he thanked god as the results were enough to harden his cock.

Twirling a finger in a turn-around-gesture, he was willing to bet she had a spank-worthy ass. Her electric-blue gaze shot to his. A flare of resentment brightened the already intense color. He resisted the urge to grin. He recognized that look, had endured it nearly every day in school.

After a moment, she did as he'd silently ordered. His gut tightened at the sight of her tight skirt stretched across her ass. Yep, spank-worthy, and Jesus Christ on stilts, her calves were shapely. The faint whistle of a train sounded in his head. He ignored it, leaned back, and drummed his fingers on the table.

"I guess you don't recognize me. It has been many years." He forced disappointment into his voice.

Jessica whipped around, head high as she glared down the gentle slope of her nose at him. "I know who you are. *Sir*."

Her acknowledgment pleased him, as did the spark of resentment rolling off her in waves. "Ah, a sub with spunk."

Jasen admitted to a bit of perverse pleasure that she was required to show deference to his Dom status, and the fact that it didn't sit well with her made him wonder whether she was truly submissive. Or was her reluctance because he'd been the nerd from high school, the one person who didn't bow to her bidding and thus earned her hatred back then.

Of course, it was more likely this was just another game in a long list of games, parties, and wasting her life on the frivolous. "We've determined we're not strangers, so back to my question. Will you accept my invitation to be my sub for the fairy tale event? I need your answer. Now." He deepened his voice, used his most commanding tone.

Jessica swallowed hard in reaction and quickly lowered her eyes, but not before he caught a hint of pure lust. His interest rose even higher. Perhaps Glorie was right in her assessment of this woman from his past. Still, she wasn't like the rest of the subs who adhered to their places and roles. If she agreed to be his sub, he accepted that he was going to have to tame this princess. He looked forward to the challenge.

"I won't ask again," he said, his voice low and soft.

"I'm thinking about it, Sir. Three days together is a long time if we do not suit one another." Her gaze lifted, slid slowly across his shoulders, and warmed his chest as she looked her fill, then boldly met and held his gaze. "You please me in looks, but—"

She put her hands behind her, fluttered her lashes, then sighed and dipped her head as though embarrassed or unsure what to say.

Her submissive pose thrust her tits out. His dick jumped from interested to intrigued. He was as aroused as he was amused, for he recognized her stalling tactics. She was attempting to lead him into fucking her tonight, trying out the merchandise before committing herself. He smiled. "Ah, you don't know if I'm dominant enough for you?"

She shrugged, the motion dragging fabric

across those hard points. "You always were bossy," she murmured.

"What was that?" His tone hardened even as his body responded to her lightly veiled challenge.

"Just saying you were good at giving orders, but of course, that was a long time ago and it doesn't mean you know how to please a sub." She sent him a calculating glance. "You could be as bad as that jerk in the lounge. Once a nerd..." One brow rose dismissively.

Her voice was soft, hesitant, the perfect demeanor for a submissive, but he knew her, knew her moves, as she'd tried them on him countless times. Once again, the game of manipulation had begun, and he had to admit, he was fascinated. She'd never left him bored. Frustrated, angry, disgusted, horny, and secretly amused. But never bored.

He stood, stepped into her space, and gripped her chin, tilting her face, forcing her to meet his gaze. Ah, that spark of resentment she couldn't hide fast enough. "What you need to understand, Miss Lowe, is that I'm a trained Dom and more than capable of both controlling and pleasing you. Question is, are you are submissive enough to suit my tastes."

"I can be a very good sub, and I'm woman enough to please you, but you can't expect me to take your word. I meant what I said. I don't know *you*, Sir. I knew *Jasen McPherson*, the nerd from school."

Jasen grinned. "Ah, you want to try me out."

Her demeanor changed ever so subtly to

satisfaction. "Are you really this clueless, Jasen? Of course, I do. Otherwise, how can I decide? You might end up being a waste of my time." She planted her hands on her cocked hips, all signs of submission gone.

Jasen lifted one brow. He wanted to laugh for there she was, in full-bossy, arrogant, and determined to get her own way mode. She made it clear she wasn't going to commit unless that committal satisfied her own needs and pleasure.

He gripped her chin hard enough to have her blue eyes go wide. "*Sir*, Jessica. *You might be a waste of my time, Sir.*"

Her lashes fluttered, then drooped to fan out beneath her eyes. "Yes, *Sir*."

His blood hummed with desire. He should dump this very, very bad idea. The smart course of action would be to retract his invitation, but dammit, she stirred something deep inside him.

"You want a demonstration of my abilities? Come with me. I shall demonstrate how I deal with subs who forget how to be respectful."

He led the way through the lounge and into the main room. Lighting was low except for spotlights on the various stations where members could engage in scenes. Small, intimate seating areas were scattered across the room. Reaching the far side, he paused at a set of doors.

The door monitor kept his features impassive, his eyes on Jasen only. "Room three is free, Master McPherson."

"I'd prefer five or seven."

"Take seven, Sir."

Without glancing at Jessica, Jasen strode along the thickly carpeted corridor. Closed doors lined each side, with an occasional open door signifying an unoccupied room. Each room boasted a window with curtains on the outside to allow monitors to check on the play taking place inside to be sure the rules of consensual, safe, and sane were observed.

Jasen paused at one open window, a clear invitation for anyone to observe. A male sub was bound spread eagle to a rack mounted to the sidewall. Stripes of thin, red lines covered his ass and the back of his thighs, and his impressive cock, sporting a cock ring, stretched out from his body.

Glorie had removed her skirt, revealing a black lacy thong with red ribbons. She stood in her red heels, applying the whip to her sub. She glanced over her shoulder, her smoldering eyes widening with amusement when she saw who was with him. She inclined her head, then reached around her partner, fisted her hand over his shaft, and bit him on the shoulder. The sub jerked his hips and moaned.

Jasen glanced at Jessica and saw her lick her lower lip. He moved behind her, cupped her tits, and squeezed, his fingers finding and pinching her hard nipples. She groaned and rubbed her ass against his erection. Her breathing came in gasps.

"You like watching, don't you, little sub?"

"Yes, Sir. I like *doing* even better." Her purr had him pulling back.

He resumed his pace down the hall, aware of her hurrying after him as he entered his assigned room. He closed the door and indicated the spanking bench in the center of the room. When she hesitated, he folded his arms across his chest. "Second thoughts, Miss Lowe?"

She bit her lower lip, but gave him the same haughty glare she reserved for those she saw as beneath her. "This isn't what I had in mind, Jasen."

"I said I would demonstrate how I deal with subs who forget their place. Did I not?"

She glared at him, crossed her arms across her chest, and tapped a foot. "I'm not in the mood to be spanked by a nerd. I prefer—"

"*Sir*. You will address me as Sir or Master. You may answer, *yes, Sir,* and then position yourself on the spanking bench. Our session started the moment you left the lounge with me. You have two choices. Do as I ordered or use the club's safe word to end the session." He walked to the bench, angling it so her ass would be higher than her head. "Do you wish to use your safeword?"

Jessica wasn't going to miss a chance to see what the nerd could do. She'd hoped for a room with a bed and restraints, but what the hell. She licked her lower lip. "No, Sir."

"Climb on, or I'll assume you want a bit of rough play and I'll put you on the bench myself." His voice was hard, all business, as was his stance. He stood, feet planted apart, looking more like an executive than a Dom in his dark slacks and white shirt. Much more sophisticated and sexy than that idiot who'd tried to force her to go with him.

She moved to the gleaming oak furniture covered with black leather and climbed on. Her knees sank into the padded knee rest, and the leather beneath her felt cool to her overheated body. She disliked being vulnerable, draped over the table with her ass in the air, which was one reason she seldom allowed her Doms to use a spanking bench. If she wanted spankings, she preferred over the knee or on her hands and knees, both positions giving her control. She gripped the metal handholds and followed the movements of his feet as he walked past her head.

"For future reference, I don't give orders more than once. If you do not obey the first time, I'll either enforce obedience or walk away. Do you understand?"

"Yes, Sir." Wow. Jessica admitted she was lost when he used that deep, rumbly voice. His tone, his words, his entire demeanor warned he truly was a real Dom, not someone who played at it or thought it sounded fun, did a little research online, and declared themselves Doms.

She could spot the fakes or inexperienced as she'd end up manipulating them, getting them to do precisely what she wanted them to do. Even many of the hard-core Doms fell at her feet. They just didn't realize it. She mentally shook her head.

Men were ruled by their dicks. And though the sex was usually pretty amazing, she was nearly always left with a sense of dissatisfaction. Her attention returned to Jasen when he trailed his hand from the crest of her bottom to the nape of her neck and along her arm.

He restrained her lower arms and wrists with the attached leather restraints. "You look good against the black leather, sub. Pale hair, red dress.

Ass in the air. Very erotic. And mine to use any way I want."

His palm roamed across her back, over her backside barely covered by her skirt, then slid along the outside of her thigh and shifted to her sensitive inner thighs. "You do want me to use you, don't you, Jessica." He urged her knees farther apart.

Air tickled her legs and rose to lick the center of her wet panties. "Yes, Sir. I want you to fuck me."

She bit back a groan. His touch was gentle, light, and fanned the flames of desire building inside her. He attached a cuff to her thigh and tightened it. His hand glided up and over one ass cheek, then across its twin and down her other thigh to fasten the last restraint.

Unlike other Doms who made quick work of attaching the restraints—if she allowed them to use them—Jasen took his time, building her need for more. Heat rushed through her and pooled deep in her center when he stroked the area just beneath her ass.

She let out a low moan as his mouth traced the path of his fingers. His breath seared her sensitive flesh. She wished she'd forgone the lacy thong. He was kneeling behind her, and she wanted his lips on her, his tongue inside, lapping her cream. God, she was getting wetter by the minute.

Cool air mingled with his hot breath. His hands skimmed her legs, lingered at the back of her knees, squeezed her calves, wrapped around her ankles, and then swept upward, easing beneath her tight skirt. She shivered at the feel of his large, warm palms smoothing over her bare skin. Air caressed her bottom when he eased the fabric up past her hips. He cupped her twin cheeks, dug his fingers in, and kissed each rounded globe.

Anticipation ramped that curl of need into an itch that desperately begged for a good, hard scratching. She still couldn't believe that Jasen McPherson was a Dom or that he'd invited her to be his weekend sub. She wiggled her hips in delight and offered herself to him. She needed so much more.

A hard nip to one cheek had her head jerking up. "Hey." Her protest ended in a whimper as a second bite sent a jolt of pure lust into her center with the force of a bolt of lightning.

"You will remain still or I'll strap you to the table. You are mine, Miss Lowe. Unless you choose to end the session."

End the session? Was he nuts? Not a chance in hell. "Yes, Sir and No, Sir. I don't want you to stop."

"Then do not move." He slid his finger beneath her red thong. The back of his nail brushed her anus and continued lower, following the thin string to the miserly scrap of fabric covering her mound. Anticipating his more intimate touch, she sucked in a breath and held it. His knuckle skimmed her damp crotch, his touch faint, like the fleeting brush of a cat's tail. He eased her panties to her knees, revealing just how turned on she'd become.

Her body quivered, every nerve heightened and on high alert. Would he use his mouth or fingers? God, the waiting was killing her. His breath on her wet pussy, he spread her cheeks apart. She heard each breath he released and wished she could see his expression. Were his eyes heavy and hooded with desire, his jaw slack? Most of all, she yearned to see him naked, see his big cock straining and begging for her pussy.

So lost in the haze of her thoughts, it took a moment to realize he'd stood and moved away without touching her pussy or clit. She blinked and felt cheated. And on fire. Her clit ached, and her breasts were swollen, the tips sensitive. She tried to twist around to see him. "What are you waiting for? Sir. Touch me, fuck me, or spank me. Anything you want, Sir."

Or do all three. She needed to feel his palm warming her ass, yearned to suck his fingers deep into her pussy, and desperately wanted his cock to claim her, to feel him pumping and thrusting inside her until he shot her into a lovely orgasm.

His silence was unnerving. What was he doing?

"You said you punish disrespectful subs. Prove it. Or maybe you're just another Dom wannabe."

She deliberately let doubt and a thin thread of contempt creep into her voice, sure, it'd earn her a smack to warm her bare ass and send delicious waves of pure need into her clit. She might not be a fan of the spanking bench, but dammit, she was here, exposed, and desperately needed him to satisfy her.

Jasen walked past her. She tried to lift her head to see what he was doing, but the restrains made it hard. As far as she could tell, he was just standing against the wall.

What the hell? "I thought you were going to give me a preview, Sir." Her voice was sulky. She didn't like lying here half-naked.

"This is your preview, Miss Lowe. Lesson one. I'm in control, and that means I give the orders. You know how it works between Doms and subs. Exchange of power. You give control to me, and in return, I'll give you want you most need. When you are ready to submit, we'll start again."

"You didn't say I couldn't talk." She pouted, and her voice turned soft and contrite. "I'm sorry, Sir. I'll be good." She hung her head as though in shame.

"Tell me, Miss Lowe, do you give orders to all the Doms? Do you manipulate them into doing what you want?" He made a tsking sound. "Haven't changed much, have you, Jessica?"

Jessica's head popped up, and she tried to stretch up. Damn, it was frustrating not to see his expression. "Why shouldn't I get what I want? You'll get what you want. Everyone is happy." The fact that he saw right through her ploys unnerved her. She felt like a child sent to a corner to think about her misdeeds—not that anyone had ever done that to her—but that's what Jasen was doing. The silence in the small room grew until she couldn't take it anymore. Tears of frustration burned. She would not cry.

Would. Not. Cry.

Would. Not. Beg.

Instinctively, she knew tears wouldn't sway this man. They'd been ineffectual ten years ago, and he'd be just as unaffected now. "Fine. If we're not going to engage in play, you can release me. I'll find another Dom to satisfy my needs." Deep inside, her mind and body protested violently. She needed Jasen to fuck her, right now. She'd wanted him ten years ago, and thought she'd finally have him, along with that coveted weekend at Pleasure Manor as Rapunzel. Guess she'd get neither.

He pushed off the wall, and in two long strides, reached her head. He knelt at face level and tipped her chin up. "Didn't take you for a coward, Jessica."

She growled low in her throat. "Just being realistic. If you don't want me, then we're both wasting our time."

"Oh, I never said I don't want you, my lovely sub. But perhaps you have a point. You need a physical demonstration of my abilities to perform as a Dom." He stood and walked behind her. She lifted her head and tried to twist her head around to see what he was doing.

Smack

"Ow!" The stinging slap to her right cheek was unexpected and shocking. "Shit! You might have warned—"

Smack-smack.

Jessica gasped as he spanked her twice more, one on top of another. She'd wanted the heat on her ass, and damn, that lovely ache deep in her center was blooming right along with the pain across her cheek.

Smack.

Now her left. "Oh-oh."

Tears stung her eyes. She bit her lip to stop herself from demanding more. She didn't want him to halt what he was doing, not when a good fucking was sure to follow. A low groan escaped as the burning heat caught her clit on fire. She throbbed, ached, and couldn't help a small wiggle in response to the lust pounding through her.

"Such pale skin. My handprints are lovely on you, sub. I'm going to turn your ass as red as your dress."

Smack-smack-smack.

Left. Right. Left.

He timed each blow, each position of his palm, so she felt the heat and burn but never went numb. It stunned her to realize he knew what he was doing. Not every Dom was good at spanking. Jasen McPherson was a master.

Tears fell even as the fire across her ass grew hotter and seeped deep. She was so damn horny and ready for him to fuck her. Moisture leaked from between her legs. He spread her cheeks to reveal her weeping pussy.

Yes, at last. To stop herself from telling him to hurry up and claim her, she bit her lower lip harder. His finger slid into the crease between her stinging cheeks and dipped into her pussy. She whimpered.

"So hot and ready for my cock. Tell me, Jessica, what do you want?"

"Please, Sir. Fuck me. Make me yours." She used her best sub voice and sighed when two fingers eased inside. She clamped the walls of her sheath around him to show how much she wanted him, how desperately she needed him.

"Ah, so wet and juicy." He slid his fingers in and out, nice and slow.

31

"For you, Sir. All for you." She gasped and cried out as he drove her closer to her release.

"Yes, you naughty sub. This is for you. Remember that." He pulled out.

Riding the storm of need, she crashed as though a large wave had tossed her onto the hard, cold beach. "No—" Her teeth mashed down on her lower lip to stop her instinctive protest. Her eyes flew open, and she saw him standing in front of the cupboards. She grinned. Sex toys. God, he planned to torment her. She loved it. *Oh boy, bring it on.*

When he returned, she eagerly anticipated the vibrator or dildo or even a butt plug. Instead, he rubbed lotion across her ass in slow, sweeping motions from one sore cheek to the other, his palm circling and caressing.

She hissed in pain even as his touch set off new waves of heat that crashed into her clit. She moaned, clenched her muscles, and then whimpered when the action squeezed her swollen clit. She was on edge, ready to come, but knew the rules. This man wouldn't allow her to get off before he gave his permission.

"You have a pretty, sexy ass, Jessica. I'm going to spank it again at Pleasure Manor. Tell me, princess, do you want me to spank your lovely ass again?"

"Oh yes, Sir." Thank goodness, she hadn't blown her chance at that coveted weekend. She felt him wiping her pussy and her thighs with a warmed wipe from the container across the room. She frowned when he removed the thigh restraints and then sighed when he slipped her panties down, lifting each knee.

He came around the front and released her arms, then helped her up and off the bench, smoothing her skirt over her sore ass. Though eager and curious for what he planned next, she kept silent and waited.

He caught her close, bent his head, and kissed her, taking control of her mouth in a sizzling kiss deep enough and hard enough to have her knees turning to jelly. A lovely buzz zipped through her system. Shit. The nerd could kiss. She swayed closer, sighing as the bulge of his erection pressed just above her covered mound. She whimpered.

When he lifted his head, she touched her swollen lips. Lust blazed from the tips of her breasts to her swollen and throbbing clit. He held her gaze, his eyes the bright green of ivy, and like the trailing, climbing plant, she felt tendrils of need twinning around her.

"I'll have your answer then. Do you accept my invitation?"

Jessica sighed. "Yes, Sir, and thank you." She lifted her arms to pull him back to her, but he stepped away.

"That's your preview. I'll see you in three weeks."

Jessica's jaw dropped. "That's it?" Her voice rose in shock. "You're going to leave me like this?" God, one good squeeze of her legs might send her over. Her clit pulsed, and deep inside, that hard ball of lust continued to expand, leaving her desperate, ready to beg.

"Yes. You wanted a preview. I gave you a

sample of both my style as a Dom and a taste of what's to come if you accepted my invitation to be Rapunzel." He handed her the red thong he'd removed. "Don't bother with panties."

"What? Wait!" She wasn't sure whether to cry or scream in frustration. "I didn't come—you didn't—"

Jasen pulled her close. The hard and sensitive peaks of her nipples rubbed against his chest and tingled, sending painful jolts slamming into her core. She sighed, gripped his shoulders, and would have shamelessly circled her hips against his erection. He wasn't unaffected by their play session. She'd make him finish what he started.

But as though he read her mind, he shook his head.

"Anticipation, princess." He dipped one hand beneath her skirt and cupped her mound, his heel pressing hard against her clit, his fingers teasing her wet slit.

She nearly shrieked in response. She was so damn hungry for him, but when she tried to clamp her thighs together to trap him against her, he pulled away.

"Jasen—Sir—I'm begging you. Don't leave me like this. Please. I need you." She bowed her head to hide tears of frustration. She ached deep in her core.

"Look at me." The command had her gaze shooting to his. The brilliant brightness had darkened, reminding her of a dark forest where the unknown lay in wait.

"Waiting and anticipation make for a bigger

payoff and reward. You have choices, princess. Find another Dom to ease your needs right now, run home and use your fingers or vibrator, or save yourself for the fairy tale event. Once there, I'll see to your every need. I promise you'll not regret denying yourself. However, be warned. Once at Pleasure Manor, it's my way, my terms. I'll not stand for your games."

Her jaw dropped. "But that's three weeks away," she wailed. God, she couldn't wait nearly a month.

He nodded and smiled grimly. "Knowing you and your need for instant gratification, I'm betting you can't deny yourself and will find someone to take care of your needs before the night is over, simply because you've never denied yourself anything you wanted. I'm challenging you, my lovely Rapunzel. Wait."

He grabbed her wrist and placed her palm against his erection. "Make no mistake. I want you bad enough to shove you to the floor and fuck your brains out. If you accept my challenge, I'll give you all the sex and fun you can handle for three days."

Damn, he was hard, and huge. The ache between her legs grew into a knot of desire. "What if I can't wait," she whimpered. God, he'd never know if she waited or not.

He stepped back and shook his head. "Such expressive eyes. Trust me, princess. I'll know. More to the point, if you give in, you'll never know how it could have been."

Jasen took one last look at Jessica's stunned expression, pleased with the combination of hunger and disbelief in her eyes, and then strode out. His dick protested violently, and his aching balls churned with need that made walking difficult. He forced himself to walk normally.

Nodding to the DM striding from window to window checking each room, he pushed open the door and left temptation behind. His cock continued to throb, the pain rising high inside him as though someone had kicked his poor, abused balls clear up into his throat.

Need swirled and made him queasy. With effort, he kept his back straight and shoulders stiff as he strode through the club. He spotted several subs, knew all he had to do was snap his fingers, head into the owner's office, and his needs would be cooled instantly. He kept walking, ignoring the sultry looks, the open invitations.

His long strides took him out into the cool night. *Fuck.* What the hell was he playing at? The sight of Jessica Lowe's red ass covered with his handprints, her pink pussy wet and hot and crying out for his cock, his fingers coated with her cream along with her breathy cries of pleasure had him coiled like a cobra ready to strike.

Three weeks.

God, he was a crazy bastard. No way would the princess from his high school days deny herself, but he'd wait. It might kill him, but he'd wait until he had her back on a spanking bench with his cock sliding in and out of her hot, wet pussy. The ache in his balls flared, and his dick, desperately hungry for her pussy throbbed painfully.

Anticipation.

The word circled his mind, the sound rhythmic, like an old-fashioned locomotive chugging down the rails. He swore he felt that metal monster breathing down his neck.

Chapter Three

Bright sunshine woke Jasen early Thursday morning. Stretching, he padded naked to a window and stared out at the grounds of Pleasure Manor. The view from the turret was spectacular with windows spaced evenly around the circular room. Built in seats lay beneath each opening while antique armoires and shelves were placed along the walls between.

He enjoyed waking to the cool, fresh air scented with sunshine, grass, and pine. Leaning on his palms, he stared out at acres of green meadow that rolled from the castle to the road like a welcoming carpet. Several deer grazed beneath the gentle warmth of the rising sun.

The next opening revealed wooded stands. From his previous visits, he knew there were small meadows, cabins, even ponds hidden inside the walls of pine. Though the forest looked wild and untamed, it was as rigidly tended as all the formal gardens. The owner, Bryce Langston, had bought the mansion and the land, then tamed it and created a place of both play and relaxation while keeping the hint of wilderness and adding to the natural beauty.

Even before reaching the next window, he smelled roses and lavender. He peered down into a garden that looked like a painting from a master. Paths shot out like the spokes of a wheel. Some led into the castle, others faded into the woods. The last window featured a stained glass insert. The work of art glowed in the morning sun. The large four-poster bed with white netting and crisp white sheets sat centered beneath the rainbow of color.

His space was one of three turret suites and included a small sitting room, bathroom, the main circular chamber, and a smaller loft in the cone of the roof above the windows. He grinned. He had plans for that space.

He checked equipment and supplies one last time, then ran his hand over the leather spanking bench. He'd decided to start his weekend with Jessica right where they left off. Anticipation exploded in his veins like an excited boy running down the stairs at Christmas to see if Santa brought him a new train set.

The dull ache in his balls spread upward, slid into a painful throb reminding him that when he'd challenged Jessica to three weeks of abstinence, he'd condemned himself to the same fate. Each day since that night had left him more desperate, broody, snappish, and unable to focus at work. His partner, who'd had enough, kicked him out of the office yesterday morning with orders not to return until he'd fucked his brains out.

The fact that his partner was his best friend and twin sister, who knew about Jessica and his weekend plans, didn't make it any easier to bear. Well, he certainly planned to fuck both their brains out, and maybe, finally, he'd get Jessica Lowe out of his system.

How had she gotten under his skin in such a short time? Better question, why had she? She was nothing to him and could never be more than a weekend of fun and pleasure. They traveled in far different circles.

He closed his eyes and ran that one session back through his mind like a movie. Almost as though she were laying there, ass bare and tipped up, waiting, begging, his palms itched to feel those nicely rounded globes in his hands and the sting when he brought his hand down on that silky-soft flesh.

His dick stirred at the memory of those pale cheeks turning red as he covered her ass with his handprints. She'd been aroused and begged for more. *Fuck.* He hadn't planned to explore her sweet pussy that night, but he'd inhaled the sharp, musky scent of her arousal, watched her cream leak and soak her panties with each smack, and when he'd pulled her thong aside, the sight of her pink pussy lips, weeping with need, had been too much. He'd given in and nearly lost control when she'd sucked his fingers deep inside her hot cavern.

He'd wanted nothing more than to shove his cock into her swollen, hot sheath, feel her throb and pulse around him as he pounded in and out until she screamed his name. But he'd had a point to make. He was a Dom and refused to allow her to manipulate him as she did so many other Doms. So he'd ended the session before either of them were satisfied.

Thumping his thumb on the leather, he

wondered if she'd waited. "Stupid to think she'd wait."

Asking her to deny her needs for a day was too long. Hell, she'd probably grabbed a Dom before he'd even been out the door. He grimaced. It shouldn't bother him, yet it did. As part owner, he could have found out, but he didn't want to know. And that was a bit worrisome.

As was the fact that he carried her photo in his cell phone, had transferred that image into each new phone for the last ten years. He couldn't figure out why, except there was something in her sad expression that haunted him. And now he had a chance to explore Jessica Lowe and see what made her tick. Another deep sigh. He didn't expect much.

Checking his email, he frowned at the bad news from one of his managers. The hotel he'd planned to hold his up-coming charity fundraiser had cancelled their event due to unexpected renovations.

"Damn." He needed a big hotel and getting a new reservation now was going to be difficult, if not downright impossible. He composed an email with a couple of suggestions and hit send after ordering a meeting for Monday morning. He copied his sister. Though he was tempted to forgo breakfast to start the hotel hunt, he turned his phone off and put it away, along with his laptop.

He gathered his clothes and strode through a cleverly hidden door that led into the tiny bathroom. He showered, dressed, and headed downstairs to join the rest of the Doms who'd elected to come the night before for a light breakfast.

****

Jessica could barely contain her glee. She was actually inside Pleasure Manor. A glittering chandelier shone onto the slick marble floor and warmed the dark, antique furniture that graced the grand foyer. An impressive floral arrangement of silk flowers and twisted twigs sat atop a gleaming cherry wood table. The quiet wealth of the foyer was both welcoming and tranquil, unlike the entrance to her father's mansion that always struck her as imposing and cold.

Nervous, she smoothed her palms down the skirt of her simple costume. The dress was a pale lavender, trimmed in a deep purple. The nearly sheer bodice hugged her breasts, pushed them up and out, and the short, flirty skirt barely covered her ass. And as instructed, she wore no panties. She didn't dare lean over even an inch.

Just thinking of what was to come had moisture gathering between her legs. But that wasn't a new state for her. She'd been in a constant state of arousal for three weeks, and if she didn't get that much hungered after orgasm from Jasen, she was going to either explode or go mad or both.

She narrowed her eyes. Well, she'd show Jasen McPherson, ex-nerd. Not only had she not found another Dom to take care of the raging lust he'd sent streaming through her body, she hadn't given in to using her own stash of vibrators and dildos. Nope, he'd challenged her, didn't believe her capable of denying herself instant pleasure, and she'd proved him wrong. Of course, she was in such a state that she could barely walk or think about anything other than sex.

"Do you have your envelope, Miss Lowe?" Hastings set his clipboard onto a small, antique table beneath a gilt-framed mirror.

Jessica handed the butler the results of her blood work. "I can't believe I'm actually here," she babbled. He smiled indulgently, his gray eyes twinkling, reminding her of a favorite uncle—not that she had any warm, kind uncles as both her parents were only children, but he was her ideal of that loving, fictional family member.

"Everything appears in order." He tucked the envelope into a file on the table and motioned for a maid to come forward. The woman in her black and white uniform carried a large silver tray with sparkling masks artfully arranged in neat rows. The butler chose one. He handed it to Jessica. "You'll wear this when you are around others. You understand the rules?"

She slid the white and lavender sequined mask over her head and adjusted it, smoothing her blonde hair that she'd left loose and long—also part of her instructions. "Yes, we use our character names among other participants."

"Correct. Remember, what happens at the castle stays at the castle." He smiled and waved her toward the closed door. "In you go. Women to the right. You are permitted one glass of champagne. Enjoy yourself."

Women to the right? Head high, shoulders back, she entered the large room and took a moment to get her bearings. The formal room held more antiques, gilt-framed pictures, and a baby grand in the far corner had been polished to a mirror-like surface. The grandeur was nothing new to her.

She'd been born to wealth. Still, she appreciated the way the room sparkled and glittered above a layer of soothing warmth. Like the foyer, this room welcomed. Soft strains of music played in the background. Couches and chairs for more intimate gatherings lined the walls, leaving the middle of the room empty. Tall windows let in natural light while two sets of open French doors allowed fresh air to enter.

She spotted a small table with flutes of champagne to her right. As tempting as it was to calm her nerves with a drink, she told herself no. She wanted a clear head to deal with Jasen McPherson.

She turned her attention to the men on her left. They formed a long line. Most stood at attention, facing the opposite wall. Her brow rose at the sight of one Dom wearing a full mask that gave him a wolfish appearance. She grinned. She'd seen him around the clubs. His identity was a mystery, going only by the name of The Wolf. His tight costume clung to every muscle of his magnificent body like a second skin.

Appreciation hummed through her as her gaze slid from chest to his crotch-less pants and the black penis glove that did nothing to hide the size of cock, which she had to admit was impressive in its natural state.

A low growl drew her attention. She glanced up and over. Ah, there was her prince in a velveteen tunic and trousers in deep purple with pale lavender trim. His eyes glittered behind his matching mask, and his lips firmed into a tight line. Was he jealous? She smiled and deliberately looked at each man. After all, how could she not look at such fine, male specimens, especially those who wore very little?

The door opened, reminding her to move away. A woman in a silky, sexy white night gown sauntered in. "Hi, I'm Wendy." She stopped to study the men. "Ah, there's my captain."

"As in Captain Hook? I thought Wendy wanted Peter Pan."

Wendy chuckled. "Poor Peter is just a little boy. Nope, I want a man, or maybe I should say, a Dom."

"Ah, Captain Dom." Jessica grinned, liking the woman. She certainly couldn't blame Wendy. Her partner's shoulders were broad, his waist narrow. He wore a leather vest that hung open and leather pants and boots. He had a magnificently bronzed chest.

"My Dom is the prince in purple."

Wendy chuckled. "He's not pleased. Watch it. You might get spanked just for looking at all these delicious men."

"God, I hope so." The two women giggled and made their way toward the far side of the room. As she passed Jasen, she smiled, wide and innocently.

He lifted his hands, rubbed them, and then clasped them in front of him. The silent reminder of his palm on her ass sent need throbbing through her. Good heavens, she might turn into a puddle right here on the floor.

She and Wendy joined two others at the far end of the room.

"I'm Alice," the blonde in the party dress with a pinafore announced, "and this is Goldie."

"Wendy and Rapunzel," Jessica introduced.

Once again, the wide, double doors opened, admitting a woman in black. She took her time sashaying past the men after snagging a flute of bubbly. Joining them, she hugged Goldie. Obviously, the two knew each other. Jessica frowned. The newcomer wore a fairy-looking costume, one that left little to the imagination. "I have no idea which character you could be."

The woman grinned and held out her arms. "I'm the Mistress of All That Is Evil, better known as the evil fairy in Sleeping Beauty. Speaking of the princess, there she is now."

Jessica smiled as Sleeping Beauty entered and chose her place in the lineup of women apart from their group. The doors opened again, admitting a tall, imposing woman wearing a costume with hearts and a stiff, stand-up collar.

"Queen of Hearts," Alice murmured.

Jessica enjoyed the light banter and speculation about the males. Impatient for the party to begin, she turned to Goldie to ask what they were waiting for. Across from her, a door opened. Three men oozed in and made her forget what she was going to ask and why.

Holy crap! From hunks to horror. Each wore white furry caps with tiny ears, studded collars, and little else except black masks and leather harnesses. They strutted toward the Doms and took their place in line.

Goldie rolled her eyes. "Subs. Doms are always

the first to arrive." She frowned, leaned forward to glance down the line of women, and then shrugged. "Don't see Mary or Bo yet."

"Ah, got it. We've had the unfortunate luck to have found their sheep." This came from the evil fairy. Everyone laughed.

"Newbie," Goldie announced, nudging her friend.

They'd all pegged Cinderella as new, and Wendy confessed that it was her first time as well. Jessica eyed another woman in blue who stood frozen just inside the door. She stared at the line of men with her mouth open. She wore a sleeveless dress with a white blouse beneath and a white apron. The skirt was nearly crotch-short in front and dipped to her calves in the back. Her dark brown hair hung past her shoulders.

The Mistress of Evil shook her head. "Definitely a first-timer." Her voice was dry. "Looks as though she might turn tail and run."

"Ah, I think we have Belle from Beauty and the Beast. Wonder where her beast is?"

"Oh, the masked wolf," Wendy guessed.

"Nope. He belongs to Red Riding Hood." Jessica recognized the exotic, dark-haired woman standing beside Cinderella as The Wolf's partner from the clubs. Her innate social graces took over. As though she was the hostess, she glided over to Belle. "You're new, aren't you?"

"How can you tell?" Belle's voice sounded high and choked.

Jessica laughed, grabbed her arm, and led her to the other end of the room. "Bunch of us are new, including me. I'm Rapunzel. Come join us." She leaned close. "We're feasting on the men from down here." She grinned wickedly. "Well, some of them."

Belle shuddered. "They going to lock you in one of those turrets?"

"I sure hope so." And soon, she hoped, eyeing Jasen as she walked past him to steer the newcomer to her group of gathered women. After introductions, more laughter, and byplay, she fell silent as she contemplated her weekend. His little demonstration told her that roleplaying with him would be different from her sessions with the other Doms.

He challenged her, and she had no doubt he'd push her. And hopefully, he'd satisfy her. One thing was certain, her time with him was not going to be boring. And that was her biggest problem. She was so bored. Bored with the clubs, the Doms, the parties. Even the few charities she chaired left her restless.

She glanced toward her Dom, met his intense gaze, and felt herself go hot and giddy. It was a sure bet he wouldn't leave her unsatisfied.

****

Jasen, along with the rest of the Doms, stood in a stoic line on one side of the parlor, unlike the women who gathered in pairs or small groups to talk, laugh, and giggle as they eyed the men like mastiffs alone with a roast on the table. Female subs continued to enter, their gazes tripping from Dom to Dom. The sexual buzz in the room was loud and thick.

The Dom to his left drew more than his share of attention. Graham Winters, known as The Wolf, looked the part of the big, bad wolf in his leathers and revealing pants. The man often met his sub in his club, making Jasen one of the few who knew who the man in the mask truly was.

Captain Hook, or Master Stuart, on his other side wore an elaborate eye patch mask that covered most of the right side of his face. The two Dom's next were twin brothers and often made up threesomes. This time around, they were two of Goldie's bears.

Most Doms at the Manor didn't care if the other Doms knew their identities as they all tended to play and use the same clubs. Of the three closest to the main parlor door to his left, two were a mystery. The third? He bit back a chuckle. He had a feeling the Evil Fairy would find herself well and truly mastered.

The doors opened. Attention shifted to the newcomer who'd simply frozen just inside, her gaze roaming the line of Doms. Surprise gave way to shock, especially when she stared openly at Graham. Jasen nearly burst out laughing as lust turned to horror when her gaze latched onto the three subs in sheep hats.

He didn't blame her and wondered if he should escort the poor shell-shocked woman to her place among the other subs. But Jessica, prim and proper socialite that she was, beat him to it. She crossed the room, head high, pose as regal as a princess, and not just for the weekend but one who played the part every day of her life.

The sheerness of her costume did little to hide her aroused nipples or the creamy swells of her breasts that weren't far from popping out of her top. His gaze drifted lower. Her skirt, short and sheer, floated around her thighs with each graceful step. The memory of what lay beneath skittered through his mind and fisted around his balls like a cruel, tormenting hand.

As though sensing his stare, she deliberately swung and tipped her hips as she passed him, revealing tantalizing glimpses of bare flesh. He'd thought her beautiful at the club in her red dress and hair piled atop her head in a fancy do. Beautiful, yes, but cold and untouchable. But here, with her long, pale blonde hair rippling down her back and swaying across the crest of her ass, she looked warmer, softer, and *shit*, stunning.

Her hair mesmerized him. As a teen, he'd dreamed of feeling those silky strands flow through his fingers like liquid sunshine. An image of her restrained, arms above her head, hair flowing over her body like a fall of water kissed by the setting sun had him sucking in his breath as though he'd just been sucker-punched.

Punched hell. The shrill whistle of a steam engine sounded in his ears seconds before his brain boiled and blew the top of his head off. He swallowed hard and shoved the image aside. Damn, the waiting just might do him in. He willed her to meet his gaze, but both women were once again staring at Graham. He fought the urge to growl again as that green-headed monster bubbled to the surface.

Her gaze swept to his. Through her mask, he felt the jolt of her bright electric blues. Heat zinged between them, scorching his every nerve ending. Oh yes, he had plans for her. Instead of running from that train breathing down his neck, he was ready to hop on and see where it took him.

He narrowed his eyes as she gave him a sassy grin and once again flipped her skirt just enough for him to see she wore no panties. The provocative sway of her hips as she breezed past sent his heart crashing to his feet, and then, as though tied with a bungee, it flew up and lodged in his throat.

Let her play her games now. Once he had her in his tower, she was his. Bo, along with her friend Mary, bounced in. He rolled his eyes. Bo's costume left her ass bare save for a red thong. The two Dommes claimed their sheep and moved to the far end of the room.

The double doors opened once again, this time, admitting another Dom. Surprised, as the Doms were required to be here before the women arrived, Jasen raised one brow. Though the Dom wore a mask, he recognized Bryce Langston, the owner of Pleasure Manor. The man hadn't participated in any of the events he sponsored since losing his wife years ago.

The gong of a clock in the far corner sounded. Everyone fell silent. The men straightened, and the women formed their line. Hastings stepped in and announced, "Queen Grimhilde."

Jasen's lips twitched as Glorie made her impressive entrance. She wore her signature leather and lace. He had to admit, she made an imposing picture in a black corset that pushed her breasts up and out. Her sheer skirt with bits of red barely covered her crotch in front and trailed the floor behind her. The powerful businesswoman certainly looked the evil queen part.

Four men, equally impressive in size and stature flanked her. Each of her guards wore shiny black boots, a full mask, and body hugging sling-style bodysuits with tight leather straps across their chests and fabric pouches to hide their dicks. G-strings left their asses bare.

A snap of her whip drew every ones attention. "Good afternoon, my lovely subjects. I'm Queen Grimhilde, Snow White's evil step-mother, and as I survey all of you gathered in this room, I declare that I am still the fairest in all the land."

She let laughter dispel some of the nerves and tension. He chuckled silently. The sexual tension was thick enough to gather and lob like snowballs.

The queen continued. "Your host, as usual, is otherwise engaged but has made available his castle and grounds. Most of you know the rules. Those who are new, your partner will explain what you need to know. You will be shown to your quarters for the weekend. We'll meet in the ballroom Saturday evening for the ball. Until then, remember—safe, sane, and consensual."

She began calling couples, starting with the Queen of Hearts who was paired with the Dom closest to the door. The second Dom in line claimed Sleeping Beauty. Goldie was next, along with the twins and one of the queen's guards. Goldie's cabin in the woods was going to burst into flames with two Doms and two subs.

Jasen mentally shook his head. There was no way he could share Jessica with another Dom. Another woman? He grinned.

Mary and Bo Peep wasted no time shooing their sheep out the door at the back of the room, the Wolf claimed Red, then Cinderella was called forward and one of the queens huntsmen lead the new sub out. Only then did he notice that Bryce, in his princely costume was gone. He smiled. Yep, Bryce was back in the game, taking on a newbie. The roles of Cinderella and her prince were fitting.

"Snow White, a word." Glorie's voice boomed.

Snow stepped forward, looking unsure. He couldn't blame her, had pegged her for another newcomer. Glorie played her part of the evil stepmother very convincingly as she trailed the end of the whip between Snow's breasts and tapped lightly.

"You, my spoiled step-daughter have been very naughty. I'm afraid there'll be no pleasure for you. Instead, you'll go with one of my huntsman into the woods. I don't expect I'll see you ever again." She gave an evil smile, then beckoned to one of the guards. "Take her away!"

His body hummed with anticipation when Captain Hook swept Wendy off her feet. He was next. He straightened, eager to claim his sub.

"Rapunzel."

Jessica hurried forward. "Yes, Mistress."

"Ah, sweet Rapunzel. *We* have some fun sessions planned for you. Even *you* won't be bored."

Jessica shivered at the look the Domme gave her along with the slight emphasis on the word *we*. She glanced down at her feet, remembering Glorie's promise at the club that one day she'd spank and fuck her. "Thank you, Mistress."

She'd tried to find out what went on during Pleasure Manor's events, but beyond being told the events were awesome and fantastic, no one gave out any details. It appeared that what happened at the mansion stayed at the mansion. Or as Hasting had put it, what happened at the castle stayed at the castle.

The regal queen walked around her, then leaned in close. "Do try to behave, little sub, though I'd love to spank that pretty ass of yours."

She swallowed hard. "Yes, Mis—tress."

Glorie faced Jasen. "Take your sub to the tower and keep her there until she learns her place."

"With pleasure, Mistress."

Jessica turned to follow Jasen then let out a squawk when he scooped her up and tossed her over his shoulder. "My skirt," she whispered, her voice a low hiss. It was so short, it now revealed not covered. Nervous giggles and outright amusement came from the remaining participants.

"Your skirt is right where I want it, sub." He strode for the door at the back of the room. Her horror grew when he ran his palm over her bare ass. Then they were striding along a long corridor, her hair almost grazing the glossy marble floor.

"Jasen! Put me down." Everyone was here for the sex, but dammit, she didn't want people to see how desperate she was. Her inner thighs were embarrassingly damp. She yelped when he swatted her ass. Planting her hands on his lower back, at the crest of nice butt, she tried to shove up. Another stinging smack had her going limp.

"Forgetting yourself already?"

The low growl of his voice along with the caress of his hand running up her thigh and over the swell of her rump sent liquid need zipping through her. Good god, she was so ready for Jasen to fuck her, she was afraid she'd start dripping like a leaking faucet. "I don't want everyone to see me naked. Put me down, please Sir."

He entered the elevator, pressed the button for the third floor. "No one to see your lovely ass but me, my sweet sub. Tell me, Rapunzel, have you been good?"

"Yes, Sir. I've been very good." Disgustingly good, and now, she was eager for whatever this man gave her. Her hands trailed down his back, enjoying the feel of strength and firmness. The sight of his nicely outlined ass made her groan. She longed to squeeze those sweetly rounded cheeks. She eased her fingers inside his waistband.

A sharp pinch to one cheek had her squealing. "Shit. Not fair. I was good. I did as you asked. I think I deserve a reward. Sir."

"How good?"

"All the way good. I didn't even use my vibrator." In fact, she'd locked her toys in her safe to keep herself from giving in during those long, sleepless nights when need raged and demanded release.

"What about your fingers? Did you touch your

clit, my sweet princess and give yourself an orgasm?" He slid his fingers between her thighs and inched them over her wet slit until they pressed against her closed labia.

She gasped. "No, Sir. I waited. I said I would, and I did." She couldn't help the involuntary squeeze of her legs. She wanted him to open her and touch her. Needed it.

"Well, what a pleasant surprise. Perhaps you *have* earned a reward." He stopped the elevator, set her onto her feet, and backed her into one corner. He fisted his hands in her hair and tugged so she met his gaze. "Mouth, fingers, or cock."

Jessica's jaw dropped. "Here?" She wanted to tell him she could wait until they got to their tower rooms, but her legs were shaking and she wasn't sure that was true. She'd never waited for anything so long or wanted it so desperately. "Sir?"

His hands glided across her shoulders and down, his palms gliding over her breasts. "What's it to be, Princess? Is your first orgasm going to be with my mouth on your clit or my fingers buried in your pussy, or do want my cock deep inside you, pumping hard and fast until you scream my name? Your reward, your pick." He eased one knee between her legs.

She sucked in a breath when his hands followed the curve of her hips and yanked her onto his thigh. *Oh. My. God.* How could she choose? "All three," she moaned as the pressure sent need spiraling through her.

"Greedy, aren't you?" He rocked her back and forth, lifting his thigh, pulling her down hard.

Jessica moaned. It wouldn't take much on his part to bring on the first orgasm. "No, Sir. Just being fair. Three weeks of denial, three choices, three orgasms. I earned one for each week I saved myself for you."

Jasen laughed. "Clever vixen. All right, princess. You get to call the shots this time. However, I have one rule. If you come before I give you permission, we stop."

Jessica sighed when he reached behind her to slide the zipper of her dress down, the sound loud. Holding her gaze, he eased the garment off her shoulders, eased her off his thigh, and let it fall and pool around her ankles.

Chapter Four

Jasen's breath caught in his throat as he stared at Jessica in all her naked glory, well except her glittering heels, which only accentuated her long, slender legs and brought the two of them nearly eye to eye.

He stepped back. God, she was a vision, both angelic and siren merged into one with her sultry gaze, full parted lips, the tip of her tongue a tease as it snaked out to glisten her lower lip. His eyes skimmed lower, and he swore steam blew out his ears as he took in the most magnificent pair of tits he'd seen in a long time. Enough to more than fill his palm, beautifully formed, and capped with rosy, upturned peaks.

His dick rose to full mast, and he yearned to lose himself in her generous bounty. Under his hungry gaze, her nipples darkened, tightened, and puckered into two tiny, tempting buds. He scooped a plump mound into each palm and closed his fingers over her warm, smooth, silky flesh. His balls tightened painfully, leaving him breathless as though someone had just screwed them into a pincer-sharp vice. Lust crashed his systems. Tingles of need started at the top of his head and vibrated to his toes and back up to rush into his cock from hilt to tip.

Torturing himself, he rolled her nipples, enjoying the way her tits swelled in his hands. Her breathing hitched into a moan. The sharp, electric blue of her eyes gave way to a blue as soft as mist floating over a lake. He tugged and tweaked each hard peak. She gasped and her lashes fluttered. He felt her delightful shiver echo through his own body. "Beautiful, princess."

Damn, retaining control was going to be a challenge when his needs urged him to claim her. What was it about this woman that affected him so?

His released her breasts and skimmed his hands down her sides, following her curves from a nipped-in waist over the swell of her hips.

"Turn around," he ordered, fighting to keep his voice even and deep. It shocked him to discover he barely got the words out.

Jessica obeyed immediately, and her obedience, her eagerness to obey, uncovered long forgotten dreams. He'd wanted this woman once upon a time, had refused to allow her to manipulate him for a few moments of pleasure. He'd ignored those desires, put them to rest, and now, his body stirred as though being awakened from a deep slumber by a beam of magical sunlight.

Lust. He told himself it was pure lust and a yearning for what he'd once denied himself. The years fell away, and once again, he was a horny teen eager for a good fuck. This time around, he'd have her and maybe get her out of his system forever.

Her baby-fine hair shimmered over her pale skin and danced across the crest of her ass. He slid his hands through the soft, silky strands that fell through his fingers like a cool trickle of water to lay ruler straight.

Shit. He was a sucker for long hair, but when it was well tended and not scraggly, he was lost. He shifted his hands and cupped her rounded cheeks.

"Spank-worthy," he murmured.

She thrust back, silently begging for more.

Hooking an arm around her waist, he hauled her against him. Each breath she drew in shuddered through him. His erection sank into the pillow of her soft ass. He tightened his throat to stop a groan and, instead, took possession of one breast while his other hand slipped down, his fingers gliding into a nest of damp, springy curls.

Her scent engulfed him, reminding him of a day at the boardwalk in Santa Cruz—cotton candy sweet, warm sun, crisp ocean breeze, and the wild excitement of riding a wooden roller coaster. Once again, his need for this woman fisted around his cock. He prayed she could hold on and not come or that he'd not lose himself in her and forget to give her permission. The last thing he wanted was to have to end this very delightful and intense session.

Mouth and fingers. He'd committed to giving Jessica two orgasms before she earned his cock and he a very long-anticipated fuck.

"Ready for orgasm one by finger?"

Finger, mouth, cock. Fuck, what had he been thinking?

Ready? She just might die if Jasen didn't make good on his promise and soon. Jessica had waited three weeks for this.

"Yes, Sir," she said, drawing in a deep breath.

His strength enveloped her, warmed her, and gave her a sense of security. For just a while, she'd pretend that she was a princess and all was right with her world. After all, she had her prince. What more could she want?

A forever prince? She chased the intruding thought away. No such thing as forever in her experience. Just now. So she'd take what he offered.

His breath, hot and moist fanned her ear. His lips closed over her lobe and sucked the flesh into his mouth. She quivered, then let out a low cry when he nipped. Need flooded her core and sent desire racing through her bloodstream.

His cock, hard and huge, throbbed against her ass and thrilled her as did his fingers poised over the heart of her sex that ached and pulsed. She thrust her hips upward, just enough to kiss the pad of his finger, and bit her lower lip to keep from crying out, or worse, demanding he get going.

"So patient, my lovely sub."

"No, Sir, but trying." She let out a squeal of pleasure when he stroked her clit with a small, rhythmic, circular motion. God, one squeeze of her legs just might send her over, but she wanted it all. If she gave in and came, Jasen would stop. The act of satisfying herself would be far too short lived.

"You feel so good, Princess. Wet and slick, swollen and eager." He licked a path from her ear to the curve of her neck and shoulder. His other hand squeezed her breast, his fingers toying with her nipple.

His voice rumbled through her and set her

nerves on edge, even as he circled harder and faster, drawing her hips into his pace and rhythm. She could barely breathe. "Very eager. Sir, I should warn you. I'm close." Her groan edged into a whimper.

"Ah, right where I want you. Will you beg, princess?"

Hell yes, she'd beg. "Whatever you want, Sir." Her heart thudded in her ears, and her hips circled faster. Each breath became a gasp. A haze of desperate need clouded her mind as her body tightened.

"Jasen—Sir—Please—"

"Please, what, princess?"

"Let—me—come." Her voice ended on a high squeak.

His lips curved on her shoulder, then his teeth grazed over the sensitive skin where shoulder and neck met. She trembled, his breathing loud in her ear. His heart pounded against her back, and his cock throbbed against her ass. It thrilled her to know he wasn't indifferent to her, that he was as turned on as she.

"Your wish is my command, this time, princess. You may come." Pressure and speed increased.

Jessica sucked in air. She'd been at the crest, ready to let go and fly, but incredibly, he shoved her higher. She gripped his arms, nails digging in, feeling his muscles jump and jitter as he worked pure magic with one hand and, with the other, he tormented her aching, swollen breast, pinching her sensitive nipples, harder, sending jolts of fiery electrical pulses deep into her pussy where he coaxed out those mind-numbing sensations with clever fingers.

Her clit swelled, her desire rose, climbed, and she tingled from nipple to clit, felt heat swarm her body from toes to head as he took all she had until she stood on her toes, perched precariously on that peak.

"Now, princess. Fly now."

He gave her no choice. He shoved her into a blood-rushing climax, one blinding, pulsing moment of utter bliss. She thrust her hips out and up, threw herself back against the hard wall of his chest, and screamed. She convulsed into a chain of spasms that shook her from head to toe. If not for his arms around her, she'd have slid boneless to the floor of the elevator.

"Oh. My. God." She gasped and couldn't hear past the pounding in her ears, couldn't breathe due to the thumping of her heart, and deep inside, waves of pleasure continued to roll through her.

"Worth waiting for, princess?"

She nodded, speech beyond her. She'd never had an orgasm rip through her, rip her into a thousand pieces. And this was just one of three? Good god, her ex-nerdy lab partner was an orgasm-giving genius.

Jasen held Jessica's trembling, shaking body tightly against him. Pure selfish lust demanded he bend her over and drive his cock inside, feel her pussy clench and throb around him. Going without sex, even his own fist, had tested his control. But he'd challenged her and, in turn, himself. Now that she was here, with him, he wasn't sure he wanted to wait.

Anticipation. He couldn't remember the last time he'd needed a woman to the point he was ready to take and see to his own satisfaction. Not since a college party where he'd hooked up with a Domme who'd had her way with him, who'd schooled him in the value of anticipation.

God, she'd been masterful and more than willing to teach a horny boy the ways between men and women. As he grew into his sexuality, it became clear that he did not have a submissive personality, that he preferred being in charge, so she'd mentored him and taught him what it meant to be a Dom and how to pleasure his partners.

Jasen swallowed his moan. Glorie had been good, even back then.

"So good, Sir," she finally whispered, stirring in his arms.

"Good, then you're ready for orgasm number two." He licked the inside swirls of her ear, dropped his voice, added, "By mouth. My mouth sucking your clit and my tongue licking your pussy."

Jessica trembled and let out a low moan. "I can wait until we get to the room," she offered, her breathing fast, her voice still heavy from her orgasm.

He grinned, then grimaced as he fought the image of spreading her out on that wide as a lake bed and sinking inside her. "Nope. You chose all three; you'll get all three right here, right now." He flipped her around and stared into her glazed eyes. Her full lips parted and begged, tempting him, but as his control was hair-thin, he snagged her wrists, backed her into the corner, and placed her hands on the handrails, one on each side of her.

"Do not move them until I give permission." Using his foot, he urged her feet far apart and dropped to his knees. "Now, where was I?"

"Mouth," she moaned.

"Ah, yes." Need roared in his ears, but he took his time drinking in the sight of her swollen clit, the tiny nub peeking boldly from her damp curls. With palms on her inner thighs, he slid his thumbs over her enticingly wet slit and up, one thumb on each side of her seam as he pulled her lips apart. The heart-stopping view of her pink, glistening flesh fried his brain and left him breathless.

Burying his head between her legs, his nose tickling by her curls, he inhaled the musky scent of her arousal. He was so lost in her, if a freighter was bearing down on him, he'd not shift an inch. He licked the drops of dew gathering, drew his tongue from slit to clit in one long, slow movement. Her cry echoed in the small enclosed elevator. His own escaped as a low groan tore from his throat. Mesmerized, caught by the storm of his own needs, Jasen tasted, sought more, probed his tongue deep into her hot pussy, and drank fully of her sweet cream as it dribbled out a drop at a time.

His. All his. His mind was a haze of pure, blinding, raw and primitive passion. Slipping his hands behind her, he gripped her ass and held her rocking, thrusting hips hard against his mouth, trapping her. She whimpered and panted with each lick, each flick of his tongue across her sensitive nub. Wanting this moment to last, he tried to keep his movements slow, deliberate, teasing, but the ache in his balls grew to a tight, painful throb. His cock, still confined, pulsed with a demand for freedom.

Finger, mouth, cock.

Fuck. He pulled back, stared at the tiny nub, her reddening lips, and imagined how his cock would feel surrounded by her sweet honey, her pulsating center, and the punch of being driven toward his own orgasm.

Knowing he couldn't wait, that he risked shooting his wad in his pants like a horny sixteen year old, he latched onto her clit with his lips and sucked. Heat stabbed into his balls and flowed hotly through his dick. Pulsating waves of desire rose like a tsunami and threatened to swamp him.

"Jasen." She shrieked his name, alternating between whimpering and crying out for more, her voice higher, thicker, each breath a whistling pant as he drove her toward orgasm number two and himself closer to the point of no return.

Faster, harder, he sucked, barely aware of her rapid panting, her mewling cries as the blood thundered between his ears and flowed like molten lava into his cock. He gasped and pulled back. "Now, Jessica. Now."

She screamed his name, thrust herself at him, and stiffened. He swore everything around him flashed white, his pleasure in hers so great. His gut clenched with each convulsion and beautiful spasm, and still he sucked, taking, taking.

Jessica rode that ribbon of electricity until her

body turned limp and shied away from too much stimulation. Her legs gave out. Jasen caught her and yanked her into his arms, her knees spread on either side of his. His mouth took possession of hers, scorched and seduced, tormented and thrilled. Sliding her hands into his thick, dark, hair, she held on and lost herself in the taste of him, the rasp of his tongue dancing and curling with hers.

She didn't have the breath to moan. Her chest burned, but when he sucked her tongue into his mouth, she decided she didn't need to breathe. If she died from lack of oxygen, well, she'd die happy.

Then he lifted his head. Air rushed into her lungs. To her dismay, he put her from him and stood. Before she could protest or ask what she'd done wrong, he ripped his tunic over his head and flung it behind him. Her eyes widened with pleasure.

Thank you, Jesus.

She took in his wide shoulders, his muscular chest, lightly sprinkled with black curls that surrounded the brown, flat discs of his nipples, tempting her to nip at one of those tiny nubs. She sighed. His bronzed skin gave testimony of his time spent outdoors. Her gaze drifted over his flat abdomen, following the narrow trail of dark hair that led, like an arrow on a map, to point where his treasure lay. Her breath caught in her throat at the sight of the engorged crown escaping from his waistband. A drop of pearly dew topped his cock like a dollop of whipped cream on a tasty treat.

Her heart raced, and all she could think about was that this was only the beginning of three days of sex. At this rate, she might not survive. Reaching up to stop him from removing his pants, she closed her hands over his.

"With your permission, Sir." God, she wanted to undress him, watch his straining erection spring out, hard and ready for one of the best fucks of her life. She didn't wait for his reply. She brushed his hands to the side, the backs of her fingers gliding across his smooth ripple of warm, bare skin. She had him unsnapped and unzipped faster than a child tearing through wrapping paper on Christmas morning.

It thrilled her to discover he wasn't wearing shorts or underwear, and the minute the zipper was down, his blatantly aggressive and magnificent cock sprang free, arrowed straight for her and bobbed inches from her lips. Saliva poured into her mouth, forcing her to swallow. Jasen, her Dom for the weekend, was everything she could have imagined or wished for him to be.

She eyed his burgeoning erection, appreciating the thickness, the ropey veins that pulsed with life, and damn, that drop of pearly dew taunted her and begged to be licked.

Shit, who knew the nerd-turned-Dom was so well blessed and would, in turn, bless her to the moon and back. She wrapped her hand around him, sighed with pleasure, and ignored his warning growl. He was her gift, and dammit, he was hers to unwrap and play with.

"Spank me or punish me later, but I cannot resist such a lovely offering." She fisted his shaft and stroked from tip to hilt, moaned at the textures of springy black curls brushing her fingers, his silky-smooth flesh, and the hardened steel beneath.

Leaning forward, she caught the dollop of his essence as it rolled from his very tip. He tasted salty, spicy, and sexy as hell, a taste that belonged only to him, a taste that was now hers. All hers. And she wanted nothing more than to swallow the head of his cock, shiny and dark with desire. She opened wide and closed her lips over him.

His swollen crown filled her mouth. She took him deep, capturing him, and using both hands, she yanked his trousers down, clamped her palms over his very fine ass, and dug into soft flesh and hard muscle.

He bucked once as though taken by surprise at her bold move. His fingers bunched in her hair, pulling her to him, not pushing her away. Jessica gave herself over to giving back to this man the pleasure he'd given her. Twice.

She sucked him deep, squeezed his plump, mushroom head, scraping her teeth over his sensitive flesh, then swirled her tongue just behind that lovely crown before swallowing as much of him as she could take hard and fast.

His groans rumbled through his chest. His fingers clenched and tugged her hair, and he thrust his hips faster and faster. Up, down, swirl, suck. She teased, gave, took, and never wanted to stop.

Earlier, Jasen had figured the top of his head had blown off. Now, it was his balls in danger of exploding. Each time he sucked in a deep breath, he was sure he'd suck his balls up into his throat. The warmth of her mouth, the rasp of her tongue, the teasing of the tip, licking, probing, and lapping, destroyed his intent to deny her—or himself—of her impromptu blowjob. God, she was as disobedient a sub as they came, and right now, he didn't give a flying fuck.

Each time she sucked him into the hot cavern of her mouth, opened her throat to take him deep, she left him trembling and helpless to hold back his groans, his gasps, and low rumblings as she shoved him toward his release.

Jolts of electrical pulses fired in a wild and crazy pattern in his brain, traveled down like lightning to strike in his balls. He curled his toes and let out a long string of fucks. The base of his spine prickled, and sweat ran down the center of his back with the effort to hold himself back. He didn't want his first orgasm with his high school princess to be a solitary experience. He wanted to join with her, feel her pussy squeeze the cum from him, and know they were one, equals and partners with one common goal.

Calling upon all the control he could muster, he freed himself from her mesmerizing attention. With quick movements, he kicked off his shoes and trousers to stand naked. Bending, he fumbled in the pocket of his pants until he found a condom, and with her hungry gaze watching, he rolled it on. He drew in a sharp breath as the feel of his own hands on his sensitized cock was nearly too much.

He concentrated on Jessica. Her eyes were a molten blue—hot, intense, and bright with desire. Her lips were fuller and redder from sucking him, and when she licked her lower lip, he felt the sensation of her tongue swirling around his cock.

He shifted behind her, knelt, and urged her onto her hands and knees, then just stared at her ass. Pale cheeks, slightly darker crease that led his gaze to the pink of her pussy. He rubbed his palms across her sweet flesh, then lifted and parted her so he had a better view. "What did I say about your lovely ass?" His voice was Dom deep and hoarse with need.

"Spank-worthy," she whimpered.

"Ah yes. Do you remember how good it felt when I spanked you, princess?" Even now he remembered how wet and turned on she'd become.

"Yes, Sir. You can spank me again." She sent him her siren's stare over her shoulder.

He was barely able to breathe his lust was so great. "Plan on it, my lovely sub. But we'll save that for the tower." He spread her knees. "I'm going to fuck you hard and fast, princess." He eased two fingers into her swollen pussy and hissed out a breath.

She cried out and clamped her muscles around him, drawing him inside. She pulsed and throbbed, and he couldn't stop fingerfucking her. He was so ready, he was afraid he'd burst the moment he buried his cock in her hot sheath. So he parted her cheeks with his left hand and thrust with the fingers of his right.

"Oh...oh. Jasen—Sir—I want you to fuck me. You said I could have your cock." Her voice rose.

"So you shall, but first, you've earned a bit of punishment." He found that rough, dime-sized patch inside her and pressed hard.

She thrust back and threw her head up. "God,

too much. Can't—stop—going to come."

"Yes," he gasped as he continued to press and rub until she shrieked his name over and over as her inner walls sucked him deeper with each spasm and convulsed around his fingers. Her cream gushed over him, and still, he kept her at her peak, lost count of her orgasms, and only when she hung her head, sagging at her shoulders, did he plunge his cock deep inside her pussy.

Jessica didn't think she had anything left to give, but the minute his cock plunged inside, her head shot up. He filled her completely, held himself deep, pushing still until she gasped at the feeling of utter and complete fullness.

He eased back out. Without him, she felt hollow, empty, and where she'd been satiated and satisfied, now she hungered for this joining. Fingers and mouth were good, shit, better than good, but having his cock embedded within her, joining them, was the ultimate fulfillment. She needed him more than she'd ever needed anything or anyone else in her life.

Before she could beg for more, he yanked himself out. Her cry was swallowed when he thrust back in, hard and fast. His groan joined hers. As though a dam burst open, he pumped his hips, driving his cock in and out.

She was so wet, the sounds of his fucking was loud in the small confines of the elevator. "Oh god, Jasen—Sir." She gasped the words as her body tightened around him, claimed him, and thrilled at the way he drove her up and higher.

"You like my cock, princess?"

"Yes, Sir." She throbbed, her pussy still pulsing from her previous orgasms. His fingers bit into her ass, yanked her hard against him as he slammed into her over and over, going so deep, she nearly wept at the incredible waves of pleasure he drew from her with the expertise of a violinist bringing an audience to tears with his gift.

Jessica had had many lovers, men she'd enjoyed or at least shared a fuck with, yet she couldn't recall a single one, mostly because none were memorable. She had the feeling that she'd never forget Jasen or what it was like to be fucked by him. That should have scared her, but instead, it excited her beyond anything she'd ever known. God, she wasn't bored with this man.

"Come again. With me, this time. Can't hold on."

Damn, she wanted to come, but suddenly, her mind couldn't take it, accept it. Too much pleasure, too many sensations, too much raw passion.

"Can't," she gasped, panicking, afraid of not being able to experience the joy of being fucked to orgasm by this man.

Jasen couldn't get enough. Her hot pussy was so swollen she was painfully tight, and his heart pounded in his ears as she squeezed him as thoroughly as her fist and mouth. Though she was wet and slick, the friction against his cock burned with incredible pleasure. He ached from his mind, which demanded this joining, to his balls drawn so tight he was afraid they might snap off, and still, his dick continued to swell and pulse with each pounding beat of his heart.

Everything inside him tightened, his body draining itself of all energy, feeling, and concentrating it between his legs. The base of his spine pricked as though a thousand hot needles had suddenly shot into him.

Shit. He wasn't going to last much longer and refused to come without her. He'd dreamed of this moment every night for three weeks, and what he'd anticipated was a shadow of the reality. Lifting his hand, he smacked the fleshy side of her ass. The sharp sting had his gut clenching. The sight of his red handprint sent his blood pounding painfully. Her cry tore through him as did the way she tightened her muscles around him.

"More," she panted. "Again."

He spanked her again and again, shocked by how intense his need grew as he fucked her hard and fast.

"I'm coming," she shrieked.

He smacked her once more and let out a roar when her pussy tightened around his dick. "*Fuck.*"

He pulled out, gasped, threw his head back, and plunged one last time, tightening his muscles, straining as cum exploded from his balls, shot down the center of his shaft, and burst out into the condom.

Her orgasm pulsed, convulsed around him, and milked him, kept him hard and straining until there was nothing left to give.

Chapter Five

Jessica woke from her short nap feeling loose and limber and eager for more. She sat, glanced around the tower, and grinned. God, their first scene had been mind-boggling. She couldn't remember the last time she'd been well and truly fucked to the point of sheer exhaustion. They'd stumbled out of the elevator and into bed like a pair of drunken fools.

So where was Jasen? The room was well lit from the windows. She judged it to be late afternoon. Standing, she wandered from window to window. A princess stuck in her tower with her prince. Just thinking of her Dom and what he'd managed to do to her in so short a time fried her brain. Even now, her body was so sensitive, simply walking teased her clit. Running her hand over the spanking bench, she sighed.

"Thinking of your punishment, princess?"

Turning, she let out another sigh. He wore a silk dressing gown of deep purple, belted at the waist. His hair was damp.

She tried to look contrite. "I was very naughty. I guess you must punish me, Sir." It was easy and natural to think of him as her Dom, not her nerdy lab partner or the boy she most hated in school. And didn't that still shock and amaze her? "Will you spank me?"

Jasen joined her, his gaze roaming over her naked body. "I do believe a spanking is on our agenda." His eyes glittered with humor. "But first, you might want a shower. By the time you're done, our meal should be here."

"That sounds good." As she passed him, he reached out and snagged her arm.

"Has the weekend met your expectations so far, princess?"

Recalling the three—no four—orgasms boiled her blood and ramped up the buzz of arousal humming through her. She lowered her gaze respectfully. "Yes, Sir. I have to admit, it's been fantastic. If I may ask, what's next?"

"If I tell you, then it won't be a surprise, now will it, Jessica."

"You're the one who said anticipation made things better. Sir."

"Ah, so I did." He tipped her chin. "Was the wait worth it?"

She grinned. "Well worth it, Sir." She'd never have believed that denial led to utter bliss.

"Are you perhaps afraid you might be bored?"

Now she laughed outright. "No, Sir. I think you've demonstrated quite well your abilities, and I can assure you, I will not be bored."

Jasen leaned close. "Just remember that, princess. I've got plans for you." He kissed her lightly on the mouth, and then straightened. He gave her a gentle shove toward the bathroom. "Go."

****

Jasen was arranging their light meal of cheese,

crackers, and fruit when Jessica rejoined him. Her hair shimmered like molten gold being poured into a mold. The sight of her naked body stirred his dick. He had a feeling he'd never tire of looking at her lush curves, pretty features, full lips, and bright eyes. The fact that she was comfortable in her nudeness around him pleased him. He planned to more than look his fill.

Unfortunately, he didn't have time to do what he wanted, so he strode to the armoire and pulled out a pale lavender dressing gown. He held it out. "Much as I'd like to keep you naked, food is here."

Jessica slipped her arms into the sleeves. "We can't eat naked?"

He ran his hands over the cool silk, across her shoulders, and then tugged playfully at a strand of her hair. "Not if we actually plan to consume a meal."

She shifted until she faced him, her palms flat against his chest. "Do we have to eat now?" Her invitation was clear.

He stared into her mesmerizing blue eyes and ran the backs of his fingers along her jaw, loving the feel of her soft skin. "I have plans for you, princess, and you're going to need your strength."

He led the way to a small, intimate seating area he'd created with big pillows on the ground and against the circular walls. A low table held their meal, complete with two candles and a small bud vase holding a yellow rose.

"This is nice," she said as she sat on a pillow, tucked her legs to the side. "The room is fantastic, and the view from up here is breathtaking. I hope we can explore the grounds or at least wander through that garden below."

"There are places we're allowed to go, including the garden, though you never know who might be there or what they might be doing." He sent her a wicked grin. "And you take your chances that I may come up with something for us to do besides stroll the paths and admire the flowers."

Yes, that idea had merit for he figured her beauty rivaled that of any of the blooms in the garden. He poured two glasses of white wine and handed her one. He tapped her glass with his. "To a weekend of pleasure."

"I'll drink to that." She giggled, held up her flute of champagne, and added a second toast. "To the nerd who became a Dom."

He lifted a brow. "And what about you, Jessica? What did you become?" He set his drink on the table, picked up a knife, and spread brie onto a cracker. He handed it to her, then fixed several more, arranging them on a plate with fruit and sliced cheese, along with a selection of different crackers.

Frowning, she shrugged. The light in her eyes dimmed, and she grew pensive. "Bored."

Jasen set the plate between them. "What do you do? Aside from parties, jet setting across the world, prowling the clubs." He snagged a slice of sharp, cheddar cheese.

Jessica nibbled on a strawberry. Another shrug. "Nothing you'd find important or meaningful."

"Try me."

"I help out a few charities; fund raising for

some of daddy's interests, stand in as hostess when he needs me for his business parties." She narrowed her eyes and set her lips in a tight line. "Don't give me that look, Jasen McPherson." She snapped her teeth into a cracker, sending crumbs onto the napkin she held beneath to keep from spilling them on the pillows.

"What are you talking about?" He looked genuinely confused.

"The one you gave me in school, like I was worthless just because I was rich." She stiffened her spine. "You probably still think I'm stupid and spoiled. I can't help it if I have money."

He heard the hurt, and yes, that thread of a whine in her voice. He cocked his head. "Money had nothing to do with how I felt about you then, or now."

"You didn't like me," she whispered.

And there it was, the same defeated, lost air as in the photo in his phone, the one that had haunted him for ten years. Back then, he'd never considered that the spoiled, rich girl was unhappy, that perhaps her life wasn't even half as good as his. In his mind, she'd had everything a teen could want—a loving father, money to buy whatever she wanted, and the other advantages he and his sister had done without for most of their lives.

"No, I didn't. You weren't very likable. Yes, you were spoiled, but worse, you acted as though you were better than the rest of us and expected everyone to do your bidding because you were rich. You used your money, your status, and that of your father's to bully and buy your way through school.

That is what I disliked. You also didn't care if you ruined my chances for a scholarship."

Jessica sighed, took a sip of her wine. "I hated school, hated the fact that girls only liked me because of what I was, what I had, and what I could give them. I learned early to capitalize on the greed of others." She glared at him. "The boys weren't any better. They never saw me, only a hot body." She arched her brows. "And yes, I had a damn hot body back then."

Grinning, Jasen nodded. "Won't argue with that, princess. You're still smokin' hot."

She wrinkled her nose. "I exploited those desires to my own ends. Except with you. You were the only person, male or female, who ever refused me anything." She set her nearly untouched drink down. "I fully admit I wasn't very nice back then. All I cared about was getting through school without having to do much."

Jasen found himself surprised to realize there might be more to Jessica than he'd given her credit for. He'd thought of her as a spoiled rich girl for so long, it was hard to believe that, in her own way, she'd been a victim of that money, her father's status, and the expectations that came with it. And a very overly protective and indulgent parent. "I suspect you managed that goal."

"Yeah. I was desperate to put school behind me. I wanted to discover life on my own, experience the excitement of becoming an adult and being free to do as I pleased."

"And what did you discover, princess?" He was genuinely interested in her response. Glorie was right in her judgement that Jessica was a very unhappy and unsettled woman. He should never have doubted the Domme.

Jessica shrugged. "Not much changed, though I didn't have to bully my way through life to get whatever I wanted. My money and reputation, then, as now, get me pretty much whatever I want." She pointed a red-tipped nail at him. "And don't ask me what I want because if I knew, I wouldn't be so damn bored with life." She hunched her shoulders and stared at a grape before dropping it back onto the plate.

Jasen put their glasses and plates on the low table and moved it out of their way. "Let me ask you this then. What do you do to earn what you have?"

Rolling her eyes, Jessica met his gaze. "Earn? I have four trust funds." She tipped her chin. "And I still get an allowance." Her glare dared him to make a snide comment.

He found himself drawn to her. His compassion and desire to help others rose and joined with a stronger need to protect and comfort. But Jessica didn't want coddling or protecting—except from herself or her parent. She needed to think and contemplate her life and find her own way out. He could help with that, after all, that was what a counselor did.

"You just hit the nail on the head, princess. You have money and power, but no ambition, no dreams, no goals. No accomplishments. I'm talking about you, personally, not your money or what your money can buy. Surely there's more out there than parties for Jessica Lowe?"

"Not really." She wrinkled her nose. "You'll laugh, but I was so bored this last year, I asked my father if I could work for him. I figured there must be something I could do, and it might bring us closer together."

"I'm impressed. I take it he said no?"

"He patted me on the head like a silly ten year old and told me I wasn't cut out for management and that his daughter was not going to dirty her hands doing menial work. He said I should stick to helping out on my little charities or go have fun and not worry *my pretty little head* over money matters. Do you know how many times in my life I've heard that? And not just regarding money. Anything of serious or important nature."

"You truly are Rapunzel locked in her tower, and your father's attitude reinforces your belief that you are useless and unimportant."

"You got it, my nerdy counselor. And it's not a belief. It's fact. F-A-C-T." She leaned forward, picked up a strawberry, and offered it to Jasen. He took it gently, his lips closing over her fingers, sucking the juice and red stain. "So what about you? I know you run a charity for homeless children and kids in crisis, most of them in foster homes."

Jasen allowed her to change the subject. It was sad to go through life with no real purpose, to just drift, and have no dreams, no hope for more, even though her money or her father's could certainly get her whatever she physically wanted. But it didn't buy satisfaction or a sense of self-worth, of doing and achieving.

He nodded. "You checked me out."

"I did. Does that upset you?"

"Nah, figure that makes you smart, princess. My sister and I were raised in a foster home. We were fortunate, had a good family. There wasn't a lot of money, but we didn't lack for anything, including love. But before the McPhersons took us in, we'd been bounced around, separated, and bounced around some more."

He reached over and fingered a strand of her hair. "The McPhersons took us in, bringing us back together. Later, they adopted us, and I swore then I'd do what I could to help others not so fortunate." Deciding to get conversation back on a lighter track, he changed the subject. "What are your expectations for the weekend?"

She shifted. Her robe parted, revealing a tantalizing glimpse of one full, pert breast. She angled her head. "Lots of sex, lots of orgasms, and lots of fun. What else is there?"

"Growth? Discovering things about yourself you didn't know?"

"You really do talk like a counselor or shrink. Which are you?" He lounged on the pillows, watching her. Her robe gaped open. The sight of her generous globes made his eyes glaze over for a moment before he realized she'd purposely tried to distract and tempt him. He reached out and tweaked one nipple hard.

Her moan echoed deep inside him as his balls tightened. Though it tested his control, he opened her robe, driven to see her. "Counselling is my day job. Kids mostly."

Jessica was woman enough to recognize the hunger in Jasen's eyes. He wanted her. "That figures. So what do you think you can teach me about myself that I don't already know?"

She wasn't sure she wanted him to answer. He already had a low opinion of her to begin with. Which hurt. And that was a shock. Since when did she care about anyone's opinion of her?

"You might be surprised, princess." He pulled her into his arms, tucked her in front of him, her back to his chest.

Enjoying the hard feel of his chest, the warmth of his body, and his clean, male scent, she eagerly awaited whatever he had in mind. At the club, he'd been so distant, so aloof,—so Dommish. But so far, he'd been a wonderful lover, very thoughtful and giving.

"Surprise me," she said, her heart racing from his nearness and his breath warming the side of her face. He crossed his arms, his palms each claiming a breast. Heat traveled from his hands to deep into her core. Her pussy wept with tears of anticipation.

"I think you're a sad, lonely princess in her high tower, put there by a parent wanting to protect you and shield you from life. Instead, he kept you in a gilded cage, kept you from exploring life and experiencing its ups and downs, and kept you from truly living. If I could teach you one thing about yourself this weekend, it would be that you have value, something within you to give to others."

Jessica sucked in her breath, as much from his words as from the way he tugged her nipples. The truth hurt. Hadn't she been trying to escape that tower her father kept her in? Wasn't she searching for more? Trying to find something to end the boredom of her life? Retreating behind a wall of haughtiness, she lightened her voice. "Why would I be sad? I have whatever I want, whenever I want it."

Yet she often wondered what it felt like to do something that made a difference in other lives. If she died tomorrow, no one would miss her, save her father, and even then, he had his businesses that consumed most of his time, and always had. Though he'd always given her whatever she wanted, he'd never given her what she most desperately craved—time with just the two of them.

"What do you have of value, Jessica? If you lost everything tomorrow, say to a fire, would you mourn the loss of anything you own or would you run out, buy all new and be as happy as before?" His hands glided over her body to her thighs.

When he spread them and placed her legs over his, she swallowed hard. The air slid deliciously cool against her heated and moist flesh. "What do you care? I'm just the spoiled, rich girl."

"Maybe I'm seeing something inside you that you can't see." His hands swept across her inner thighs, easing higher, inch-by-inch until his thumbs brushed her aching clit. His fingers rested on either side of her wet slit. "Answer me, and I'll reward you."

She stared at his tanned hands, her sex nestled in the vee between thumbs and forefingers, framing her damp, pale curls. Blood pulsed beneath his touch, and her lips were plump and eager for his touch. Her gaze shifted to her smooth, creamy legs draped over golden-brown thighs. Light and dark. Rich and poor? No, there wasn't anything poor about Jasen, and never had been.

There'd been plenty of kids in school who wanted to be her friend just to get whatever she dangled over their heads, but not this man. And he'd given her one of those things she valued. Because he'd refused to do her work for her, she'd earned an honest grade in their shared class and she valued that piece of paper with her "A". But she wasn't going to tell him that.

"I have a ratty stuffed dog that my mother gave me before she died. My nanny threw it away because it was dirty and old. I cried. She said I had lots of nicer toys. I snuck out and got it out of the trash and kept it hidden."

"Was that so hard to share?" His middle finger eased into her, drew her cream up through the seam of her lips and over her clit, over and over, slickening her.

Watching, she became mesmerized by his strong finger dipping into her, stroking her. He opened her, revealing the heart of her desire. Hunger struck her belly, leaving her feeling almost faint, as though she'd not eaten in weeks.

"Use your fingers, princess. Let me watch you come."

On edge, waiting and anticipating his fingers moving over her, she blinked. "Me?"

She wasn't a prude, had certainly gotten herself off with her partners before, but only when they couldn't do the job without her helping things along. For the weekend, she'd expected him to pleasure her. Again. *Mouth, fingers, cock.* God, she wanted all three, again and again.

Jasen rubbed his cheek against Jessica's hair, loving the silky softness. "Share yourself with me. Give yourself to me and let me watch you bloom."

The urge to touch her, rub her, and send her back into ecstasy was an irresistible compulsion, but if he touched her, he wouldn't stop, like in the elevator, he'd be tempted to use his mouth on her, his fingers, and he'd finally do what he wanted above all else, he'd fuck her with his cock. His dick screamed yes, but his pleasure had to wait. They had places to go, things to do and see before the night was over.

His breathing hitched when she hesitantly covered her clit and stroked. "That's it, princess. Nice and slow. Tease me, make me want to lift you and shove my cock into your pussy."

She gasped and groaned. "I want to ride your cock."

"You'll have it. Later. Show me how wet you are." He sucked in his gut when she dipped her middle finger into her pussy. She pulled her glistening finger out. Unable to resist, he snagged her wrist and sucked her cream.

"You taste good, my lovely sub. Continue." He released her and lost himself in the sight of her swelling clit, mesmerized as she stroked and circled. "Faster."

She panted and moaned, pushed back into him as she humped her fingers, her hips circling harder and faster. She squeezed her muscles, popping the tiny nub out of its protective hood. He loved the sounds she made, her breathy mews, the cries trapped in her throat, and her loud gasping breaths.

"Come for me, princess. Share your pleasure with me," he murmured in her ear, feeling her gathering herself in preparation. She tensed, her clit stiffened, strained, pushed against her finger. Everything inside him flashed white-hot.

He couldn't breathe, couldn't take his eyes off her, and when she let out a low, hoarse cry and convulsed as her orgasm swept over her and through her, Jasen couldn't hold back his own moan of pleasure. Her willingness to share herself with him, to come *for* him not *because* of him, pleased him, maybe more than it should have.

Holding her close, he waited for her body to relax, her hands falling aside. "Beautiful, princess. Thank you."

She got to her knees. "What about you? Can I pleasure you now?"

The thought of her hot mouth swallowing his cock made him groan, but he shook his head, wishing they had time. He stood, conscious of his pulsing erection and aching balls. "Go wash up and return here. We need to go."

Normally, he'd have taken on the delightful duty of washing and cleaning his sub, but he didn't dare touch her. Not yet.

He winced at the uncomfortable tightening of his balls. Walking was going to be hell. Fuck, until he was able to drive his cock into her pussy, he was going to be on edge, his control tested once more.

****

Returning to the room, Jessica found Jasen standing at one of the windows. "Where are we going? And what do I wear?"

He strode over to her and adjusted her robe. "What you're wearing will do nicely." He stepped away from her. "Show me you are ready to assume your submissive role, princess."

His voice hummed through her like hot lava, leaving her burning and tingling. Most Doms left her cold, but not Jasen. His demeanor had her instantly complying. She thrust her shoulders back, clasped her hands behind her, and stared at her feet.

"Very good, princess. We are joining a few other couples for some entertainment. Once we leave this room, I am in charge. While we are among others, the rules of Dom and sub apply. You will obey and do what you are told. Do you understand?"

"Yes, Sir," she murmured. "If I don't do what you ask, I'll be punished." And probably in a most delightful, exciting manner, which made it even more tempting to disobey.

He tipped up her chin, his eyes green chips of sharp glass. "Not this time, Jessica."

He'd used her name gently and tenderly several times during their afternoon together, but now his tone was harsh. His whole stance shifted from relaxed and caring to forbidding.

She blinked in both confusion and surprise. "Sir?" She couldn't address him as anything but Sir as he was suddenly all commanding Dom.

"If you do not obey, if you forget your place, it's game over and the weekend comes to an end for you."

Her arms fell to her sides, and the spit in her mouth suddenly dried up like water in a desert. End? She licked her lips. "Have I not pleased you, Sir?"

Surely, he'd enjoyed their time together so far? Hurt that he'd threatened to end their weekend, she bit her lower lip and fought the prick of tears.

"You have more than pleased me." His tone softened.

"I don't understand," she said, afraid of doing something to displease him and have him tell her it was over. In that moment, she realized that nothing was as important as having this man for these three days. With him, she felt alive, and more importantly and scarier, he understood her, better than she understood herself.

"We will be with others, and I won't tolerate games or manipulations."

"You're afraid I'll embarrass you?" She pushed the line with most Doms, driven by her sense of absolute boredom.

"No, princess, I don't want you to embarrass yourself." He cupped her face between his large hands. "Tonight, I'm going to push your boundaries and ask a lot of you. I'll expect more from you than anyone has ever asked or demanded. In return, I guarantee you will not be bored, and perhaps, you'll make some new discoveries about yourself and your sexuality. Can you trust me and put yourself in my hands, give me your all and not hold back?"

Nervous, she considered. In her dealings with other Doms, she did only what she chose, too afraid to let go. What did he have planned? Could she give herself totally to this man, something she gave to no other? Yeah, she could. Jasen was different, or maybe she was different with him. She was comfortable with him, relaxed. She realized she could be herself, not just some rich sub looking for a night of fun.

Slowly, she nodded. "I trust you, Jasen, as a man, a friend, and my Dom."

God, was he her friend? He'd taken time to talk to her, get to know the real her, and shared his own past with her. Friends did things like that, right? Suddenly, she yearned for this man's friendship. And his respect. She couldn't demand either, nor could she buy that respect. If she wanted more from this man, she'd have to earn it. For the first time in her life, she had a goal.

"Thank you, Jessica. That is your gift to me. Tonight is my gift to you." He led her to the armoire and drew out the masks they'd worn earlier. She slipped hers on.

Once again, he tipped her face to his. "You have a new safeword for tonight."

"Sir?" She trembled.

"I quit. That is your safeword."

"Quit as in I'm out?"

He nodded. "Yes."

She narrowed her eyes and firmed her lips. "I'm not a quitter, *Sir,* and I won't embarrass either of us." And she'd show her nerdy lab partner she was capable of putting others before herself.

"Good girl," he murmured. "Let's go."

She nodded, then followed him out of the tower

room, down a narrow, curved staircase, then along a long, marble corridor. They entered a large formal room that had to be a ballroom with its arches, a domed ceiling with an old world mural, and huge chandeliers dripping light.

He led her to the far end. She spotted a circular stage set into the gleaming wooden floor. Spotlights shone on a spanking bench with knee rest. Curtains formed a triangle, like a wedge of pie with a slice missing.

Spread in front of the stage were separate seating areas with pillows, low padded benches, and covered baskets arranged on thick, yoga-style mats. Each was spaced equal distances apart, each close to the stage. Planters filled with topiary and ivy acted as dividers.

She'd been in enough clubs and private gathering to recognize that there was going to be a demonstration taking place on the curtained stage. Her blood hummed with excitement as she enjoyed watching, and judging from the setup, the audience would participate in some personal enjoyment as well.

Jasen led her to the only unoccupied seating area. Curious and excited, she noted that Wendy and her Dom were to her left. To her right, Alice lay across a bench, her partner behind her, a bullet in his hand, his fingers sliding in and out of her pussy. Jessica went hot all over and quickly glanced at Goldie on her knees, sucking the cock of a masked man lying on his back on the bench. One of the other men with her had his hands on her ass while the third watched.

"Holy cow," she whispered.

"Does it turn you on to see Alice ready and eager for whatever her Dom chooses to do, princess? Or Goldie and her partners warming up for the evening's activities?" Jasen's voice was a low murmur in her ear as he urged her onto her knees.

"Yes," she breathed the words, her voice hushed. She could still see her neighbors over parts of the low planters or between them. They, too, were partially shielded, but not totally. She heard noise to her far left and spotted Hastings pulling a room divider from one of the thick, vine-painted columns that rose to where the ceiling curved to meet wall. From the other side, a woman in a maid's uniform pulled the other half of the divider from the wall. They met in the center, fastened the two sections, enclosing the participants.

"How clever," she exclaimed and then covered her mouth with her hands. "I'm sorry, Sir," she whispered.

He grinned. "It is. The club often holds demonstrations and classes in here. We'll return here for the Ball Saturday evening."

Magical. She could easily imagine herself in a make-believe castle where the unexpected occurred.

Jasen reached over and drew the basket close. He lifted the towel, and her brows shot up at the sight of so many sex toys. The lights above winked out, and tiny, white lights dotting the plants flicked on.

Oh yes, magical.

Behind her, he untied the belt to her robe, eased

the silky fabric off her shoulders, and set it aside. He pulled her into his arms.

The sharp click of heels drew her attention. Glorie entered the demonstration area from a side door. Her two huntsmen followed and stationed themselves on either side of the stage. A spotlight hidden high above flipped on, illuminating the stage. The Domme had foregone her favored black and red and, instead, wore a gold and black lace corset that pushed her breasts up and out.

The sheer fabric hid little. The corset ended in two sharp points, drawing the eyes to a small, golden triangle in front and a thong that cut between her most queenly ass. It joined a wide swath of black lace with a gold bow just above the base of her spine. She walked on golden, icepick heels that glittered in the light spilling from above. The woman had to be one of the most regal, sensual, and beautiful women Jessica had ever known.

Glorie stopped center stage and smiled. In her hands, she held her customary riding crop. "Welcome, my lovely Doms and subs to our little demonstration of various BDSM techniques. Tonight, you'll be both entertained and educated, as well as the entertainment and teachers. Part of the Dom/sub relationship is pushing boundaries and comfort zones, and not just for you subs. This applies to Doms as well. For many of you, Doms included, tonight will accomplish both."

Gasps of shock filled the air as understanding dawned. Jessica whipped her head around and stared at Jasen with mouth parted. His eyes glittered behind his mask, and his stance, stiff and unyielding, dared her to protest.

Accept or quit.

He didn't have to say the words. They were unspoken. Heart pounding, she returned her attention to Glorie. While she liked watching, she wasn't sure she wanted to be watched in turn.

Jasen leaned close, his lips brushing her ears. "I said you wouldn't be bored, princess, and who knows, you might find you like people watching you."

Magical, hell. This might prove to be pure heaven. *If* she could go through with it.

Chapter Six

One day, Jessica Lowe, I'll spank that lovely ass of yours, and then I'll fuck you.

Recalling Glorie's words sent alternating waves of heat and icy chills skittering down her spine, arrowing deep into her core, then flaring into her pussy. She quivered, the recently sated ache between her legs now turning traitor as her body came alive at the thought of Glorie carrying out her promise.

"She's going to spank me in front of everyone, isn't she?" She whispered the words as Wendy and her partner joined the Domme. Captain Dom was restraining his sub on the bench, positioning her bottom higher than her head. The spotlight focused tightly on the three on stage.

"You bet your ass, princess." From behind her, his hands closed over her breasts.

The idea of Glorie spanking her scared her as much as it turned her on. "*Oh. My. God.*"

Jasen chuckled, his breath warm against her neck. "You're going to be the star in your own live porn show. While you're front and center, everyone will be watching."

She gulped. "I've never done something like this. What if I can't come in front of everyone?"

"Aside from the fact that you are so sexy and

responsive, you'll also be well primed, princess. I bet you're already wet just thinking about it." He leaned forward, urging her onto the knee-high bench. He spread her legs and slipped a finger inside her pussy. "Ah, very wet indeed."

She bit her lower lip to keep from moaning. It shocked her to realize he was right. Hadn't she always wondered what it would be like to have people watching her while she was being fucked? The monitors at the clubs checking on the play in the rooms didn't count as they were mostly invisible, and she'd never been brave enough to volunteer to take part in any of the demonstrations.

Jasen removed his fingers, leaned over her, his body blanketing hers, letting her feel his erection slide through the crease of her ass. He slipped her mask off. "We're in shadows. I want to see you. This is going to be a night of orgasms for you, princess. Are you up to it?"

Groaning softly, she glanced over her shoulder. "Bring it on."

"Good. Let's have some fun, shall we?" He kept his voice to a low whisper. "First demonstration is back door play. Do you like being fucked in the ass?"

"Only if done right," she replied in a low whisper.

He shifted off her, and Jessica returned her attention to the front of the room. Glorie pulled forward a board on wheels. Various butt plugs in different sizes, colors, and shapes formed a colorful display. There was also a nice selection of dildos and anal beads.

A small table set to one side held bottles and tubes. Glorie was explaining the various types of lubricants and their uses. While she talked, Wendy's Dom demonstrated by applying lubricant liberally to his sub while working his finger into Wendy's ass.

Jessica sucked in a deep breath when cold lube hit her overheated flesh and she realized Jasen was going to engage in some back door play of his own.

"Aren't we supposed to be paying attention to the show?" She drew in a sharp breath of air when Jasen mirrored the movements on stage.

Her heart raced, and she was glad spanking was to be her demonstration. She wasn't sure she'd have been able to do what Wendy was doing. She shivered with anticipation as Jasen's finger glided in and out. Would he take her there with so many people so close?

"This is group participation, princess. They demo, we play along." Applying more lubricant, he worked two fingers inside. She tipped her ass up and pushed back, gasping at the slight burn of her tight muscles stretching. The pain morphed into pleasure as he stroked sensitive nerves to life. She couldn't remember the last time she'd engaged in anal sex, and seldom was it something she enjoyed. Jasen just might prove to her that it really could be good.

She breathed deep and tried to relax as he massaged and stroked until she accepted his intrusion. "Feels good," she panted.

Pleasure hopped from ass to clit like a flat rock skipping across a calm lake. Her attention wavered between what Jasen was doing, her body's reaction, and the stage where Glorie removed several toys from her display board and held them up. She discussed the attributes of each, including the ones with built in vibrators or vibrating bullets. She held up an item that allowed a man to penetrate both ass and pussy at the same time.

Jessica trembled at the idea of Jasen filling both her holes as he fucked her. As though he read her mind, he slid two fingers into her pussy so both cavities had a taste of pleasure, yet not enough to satisfy. She wanted so much more.

"Does this turn you on, princess? I bet you'd like me to fuck your ass and pussy at the same time, wouldn't you?"

"Yes," she mumbled, struggling to keep from crying out.

His fingers stroked in tandem. The two in her pussy shoved in, the two in her ass pulled almost out. Pulling and pushing as though a string or ribbon connected his hands and each movement slid invisibly across clit and through her slit. Her hips danced, swayed, and circled, begging for more. When he removed his fingers, she dropped her head to the bench, gasping and panting. Drawing in deep breaths, she tried to calm her pounding heart.

"Watch," Jasen commanded.

On stage, Glorie had chosen a long, purple, anal bead toy with at least five graduating beads on the long wand. She handed it to the Dom, and as he eased the tip with the smallest bead inside Wendy, Jessica groaned and flushed hotly. God, she wasn't a prude by any means, but she was glad they had a small modicum of privacy. No one could see the combination of fascination and lust along with sheer embarrassment on her face, though from the sounds coming from Alice, privacy was an illusion.

Wendy's Dom inserted the second bead, then the third before pulling it out to start over. His fingers spread her cheeks so the audience saw the way her tight rosette opened, then contracted around the bead.

Something hard probed Jessica's thrumming anus, and she realized Jasen had the same toy. God, it was totally erotic not only to see the demonstration in front of her, but to feel the actions mirrored in her own ass.

Jasen's gut clenched each time Jessica's tight ring of muscle bloomed open, then swallowed a bead. By the fourth, his cock was pulsing, and his balls had flown up into his throat, making breathing difficult. His princess had a lovely ass with plenty of flesh. He preferred a woman with a rounded bottom, not an anorexic body of skin and bone. Like Wendy's Dom, he held Jessica's cheeks open with one hand while easing the anal beads in and out until her body swallowed all five beads. She moaned and wiggled in delight as he pulled them out, then eased them back in.

Glorie stepped forward. "This beauty is a vibrating finger anal rimmer. It's a nice little toy, good for teasing and tormenting your sub. Use it on your finger or choose a model that leaves your hands free to explore other pleasures."

She held up a small, two-inch mini plug that fit on her forefinger. She smiled wickedly as she indicated the display board with the grace of a game show hostess. More rimmers, in various sizes were mounted.

Jasen picked up the medium size, slipped it onto his finger, and at the same time as the Dom on stage, he added more lubricant and eased the narrow end into Jessica's contracting anus with short, slow strokes. He only half watched the couple on the stage, his attention on the muffled moans coming from his sub, the way she wiggled her delectable ass, and the erotic sight of her opening to take the toy inside. He flipped the built-in bullet on.

She squealed with shock and panted when he pushed it home. Soft gasps sounded to his right, followed by a tight, high cry. He leaned over her. "Do you hear Alice? She's enjoying the show." He pumped the toy in and out, alternating slow strokes with fast.

"What's not to enjoy?" She moaned as he wrapped an arm around her waist and yanked her off the bench, positioning her in front on him on her knees.

The vibrations of the plug traveled through his cock. He jerked in response and tortured himself by parting her cheeks and stroking his dick along her wetness, the tip of his condom-cloaked cock poised at her entrance, the thin latex keeping their juices from mingling. Shit. He wanted to drive himself home, but he had rules he was required to follow and it wasn't his time. As in the elevator, the evening was going to test his control.

Glorie once again commanded their attention. "As you lovelies can see, Wendy is enjoying our demonstration. On to our last method of enjoyable anal play.

"Ah," Jasen whispered in her ear. "For subs who want double penetration, but not two partners."

Jessica licked her lower lip when Glorie held up an orange dildo shaped like a cock with a cock ring attached. She handed it to Captain Dom. Jessica's heart raced as she watched the Dom on stage lubricate himself and ease his cock through the ring. He stepped behind Wendy. The table was angled so the audience had an unobstructed view.

Jessica let out a moan when Wendy's Dom parted his sub's cheeks, removed the plug, and added more lube to her glistening anus. He slowly worked his cock into her ass and, at the same time, eased the dildo into her pussy.

"Oh-oh." Jessica pressed her ass against Jasen's hard cock, as though inviting him to take her. Wendy's gasps, moans, and cries of pleasure grew.

Jasen cupped Jessica's breasts, his fingers pinching and tugging her nipples. "Want to try this later, princess?"

"Need you ask?" Her nails dug into his thighs. "Why not now?" God, she wanted his cock inside her, wanted him to fill her totally.

He chuckled, and then groaned at the thought of his rod gripped by the tight ring of her sphincter. As much as he yearned to engage in his own back door play, he resisted. "I'm saving myself for the finale. But there's no reason for you to wait." He fished out a clit tickler from the toy basket, flipped it to high, and then pressed it against her clit. She clapped her hands over her mouth to smother her scream.

He nibbled on her ear lobe. "Let's show our stars how much you're enjoying their demonstration. No need to be quiet," he ordered, holding her firmly when she bucked, groaning each time her ass bumped against his aching dick.

Jessica took him at his word. When Wendy let out a shriek on stage, followed by her Dom's shout, she, along with the other women and one male, joined the starring couple with their shouts of release. Jasen's pride and pleasure in his princess grew. He kissed the hollow of her neck, murmuring soft words of praise as she calmed.

Jasen lifted her and held her against him. She let her head fall back on his shoulder and opened her eyes. Wendy was being cleaned by her Dom. He talked to her in a low, soothing voice, then released the restraints and carried her back to their area. Jasen had removed both toys and, with a wet cloth, washed and dried her. He flipped her around, pulled her close, and kissed her hard and deep, his tongue sweeping inside her mouth and stealing her breath.

Jessica sucked his tongue, held him prisoner, his hot, spicy scent and warm mouth as arousing as his fingers and cock. She moaned, shifted her hips restlessly. Her need for this man was a bottomless pit and that both scared and excited her.

When he lifted his head, his gaze held hers captive. "That was very good, just the first of many, I promise."

Barely able to breathe, let alone think, she stared up at him. "What was good? The kiss or the orgasm or the demonstration." In her mind, all three were magical.

Jasen's thumbs caressed her cheeks, then glided across her lips. His grin was both wicked and hot. "The demonstration was good, the kiss hot, but your orgasm wins out on this contest, and I promise, the next one will be even better.

"Good god, I might not survive another." Yet she couldn't wait for more. Of everything.

Behind her, Glorie announced the next demonstration on erotica spanking. "Spanking, when done correctly, offers pure physical pleasure and, for some, a thrill that comes from engaging in an activity many consider taboo. Our next couple please. Rapunzel and her prince. To the stage."

Jessica gulped. God, it was almost her turn. She leaned her forehead on Jasen's chest, seeking courage, trying to block Glorie's voice. She enjoyed being spanked but only with a palm and never in front of others. Jasen was good, and she had no doubt Glorie was a master, but she was afraid she'd freeze and not be able to come, that she'd just cry and make a fool of herself.

Jasen tugged on her hair, tipping her head back. "Ready?" His voice was low, his gaze searching.

Jessica bit her lower lip, unsure.

"Two choices, princess," he reminded.

Quit or participate. She drew in a deep breath and nodded.

"Good girl." He slipped her mask on and indicated for her to take her place on stage.

She wished he'd take her hand and lead her but realized he was forcing her to make the choice and take charge of her own actions and decisions. She'd have no one to blame or accuse later if she walked up there on her own. She stopped before the stage where a spanking horse and display board of whips, floggers, and paddles replaced the anal scene. She swallowed past the lump in her throat. She had her own movie set.

Glorie stepped forward, drawing her attention by using the tip of her riding crop beneath Jessica's chin. "Very brave, sub. We'll take good care of you." She swept a hand toward the padded bench.

Jessica took those final steps, her heart pounding, partly from fear of the unknown, but mostly from pure, unadulterated lust. Part of being a sub was giving herself willingly to her Dom, in this case, to Glorie, who was both hostess and queen of their fantasy world. And Jasen, as her Dom, had the right to ask her to do this. After all, he'd given her the choice back in their room.

Participate or quit.

Though Wendy's Dom had done the demonstrating and fucking and their demonstration was chili-pepper hot, Jessica wasn't sure she could perform in front of so many others. But she wouldn't let Jasen down. Pride had her squaring her shoulders, and with head held high, she drew in a deep breath and draped herself over the padded horse. Unlike the spanking bench Jasen used at the club or the one Wendy had graced, this one resembled a vaulting horse, forcing her to assume a position much like bending over to hold her ankles.

Jasen's gaze was transfixed on his sub. The spotlight shone on Jessica, caught in her hair and gave her an almost angelic appearance, except angels wouldn't be naked and splayed so erotically. He stared at her sweetly curved ass, her pale, blonde curls that were nearly translucent and couldn't hide her swollen reddening lips or her sweet, pink pussy. He ran his finger down one ass cheek, dipped into her crease, and continued. Beneath the lights, he could see the way she pulsed, as though seeking to draw one of his fingers deep inside.

Blood pounded in his ears and echoed in his cock. He was afraid his thumping heart just might burst from his chest. His princess was so damn wet. Her lower back arched as she silently begged to be spanked. And fucked. And he wanted nothing more than to oblige her. *Fuck.* He had one thought, and that was to fuck his sub, feel her swollen cunt swallow his cock, and trap him in her moist heat as he pounded his rod into her drenched pussy until they were both screaming and shouting their release. But he had to wait.

Glorie cleared her throat. His gaze shot to hers. She wore a wicked smile on her red lips, letting him know she knew just how desperate he was. She jerked her head toward the front of the spanking horse, then continued her instructions by holding up a paddle and explained how to use it.

He walked around and knelt to fasten the cuffs to Jessica's wrists, then arranged her hair to one side so he could see her face. She opened her mouth to speak, but gasped when the queen rubbed a paddle across her ass to demonstrate where and how to spank. Jessica let out a yelp when the Domme smacked her twice on her bottom.

"That hurt," Jessica whispered, eyes wide and

watering. Tears, nerves, and lust swam in her eyes. He knew she never allowed any Dom to spank her with anything but his hand. Her spunk, courage, and spirit formed a hard knot in his throat. He knew what it cost her to submit to Glorie in a public setting.

"I'm proud of you princess," he whispered. He drew her attention to his straining cock. "I don't normally put myself on display. There's no hiding the fact that you turn me on or that I want you to the point of great pain. I'm suffering right along with you."

For this weekend, he'd had a choice. Participate in Red Riding Hood's outdoor scene where they'd have been part of a group but hidden and out of sight while Red's fantasy played out and she was fucked with an audience watching. Or they could take part here, where things were public and voyeuristic, where they were required to watch and be watched.

Both Glorie and Bryce felt his sub might get more out of this activity than the other. As Glorie had said, Jessica wouldn't be bored. So he'd taken himself out of his comfort zone as well. He had to admit, they were right as usual. With two more shows, the evening was just beginning.

Glorie called his name, and he took her place as host while she prepared to spank his sub. He wanted to be the one doing the spanking but part of this act was to fulfill Jessica's fantasy of being spanked by the Queen. Glorie had an uncanny sense of others and their deepest desires. He stood and nodded to Glorie.

Chapter Seven

Jessica wanted to call Jasen back, ask him to stay with her, hold her, but she understood what it meant to be submissive, even if she wasn't always a good sub. Glorie demanded both her submission and her acceptance. She was sub to the queen Domme. At least for this part of the evening. *Holy shit.*

Ah, sweet Rapunzel. We have some fun sessions planned for you.

We. The queens taunting remark in the parlor made so much sense now.

To her surprise, Jasen began talking about the attributes of floggers. *Damn.* Conflicting sensations welled up from deep in her lower abdomen—anticipation and dread. She accepted it was both sexual and emotional, again part of being submissive.

And while she'd fantasied about being spanked by Glorie, she'd never imagined it would actually happen. She hadn't said anything, so how had the woman found out? And now that she was in position—ha-ha—to have her fantasy realized, she was as nervous and hot as a cat in heat.

The teasing dance of leather strips bouncing up and down her spine then trailing over her ass had her squeezing her eyes shut as she waited for the sting of pain. Again, Glorie administered two strokes, each applied expertly, leaving only a small sting of pain.

Jasen moved on to whips. As he talked, Glorie touched Jessica, alternating between light caresses and brushing the tip of her riding crop along the sensitive flesh beneath her cheeks. As she had with paddle and flogger, she demonstrated the whip. The swishing sound along with the thin snap to her ass had Jessica crying out.

Tears sprang at the lines of pain flaring across both cheeks. *Shit.* The burning was much more intense, seeping deeper, faster. She tensed and pulled at her restraints until Glorie ran a soothing hand over her ass.

"Very nice, sub," she said, speaking softly, encouraging the pain to sink and spread.

Swallowing back her instinctive protest at the unexpected praise, Jessica worried her lower lip. She couldn't do this, had never done this, yet before she could protest, the discomfort changed to intense need. Shocked, she felt fluid seep from her pussy. God, not only was her body hot and turned on, everyone in the audience could see she was aroused. Her embarrassment deepened when Glorie parted her cheeks.

She choked back a cry. She'd never had another woman touch her so intimately, and it both excited her and scared her to admit her body was humming with a burning lust that threatened to consume her every thought. She wanted the Domme to finger her, stroke her, and good god… Did she want the woman to fuck her? Her heart pounded, her clit pulsed in response, and she shivered in anticipation. Sensations strolled from ass to her center where she still throbbed from her last orgasm. She couldn't help arching and wiggling.

Jasen chuckled. "My lovely princess is aroused, demonstrating that the bottom is a hot, erogenous zone." He joined Glorie and ran a palm across Jessica's ass, stroking the burning embers. "Here is what we call the tender zone." He caressed the lower cheeks and upper thigh. For you subs, this is a sweet spot. Spankings here often result in an orgasm with spanking alone."

Jessica moaned, unable to believe she was actually enjoying being on display and being spanked in front of others. Just imagining the others in the audience being as turned on and hot was enough to make her wiggle her ass, silently begging for more. She heard the queen's heels clicking on the wooden stage.

"I'd like to add that many couples like to spank on other areas of the body—breasts, clit, and across the anus."

"No way" Jessica's head shot up.

A sharp tap to her ass with the riding crop had her dropping her head. She heard Jasen's low chuckle at the silent but effective reprimand. *Shit.* She wished she could see him, let him know this might be too much, but her choice was to submit or quit and there was no way in hell she was quitting.

To her relief, Jasen continued. His warm hand rested on the crest of her ass. "Let's move on to the most common form of spanking. The hand."

Jessica wasn't sure she was relieved or not to

know they were done with whips and floggers. As he spoke, Glorie slid her riding crop between her cheeks. Heat flooded her system and rushed to pool between her legs. She was so damn wet, she felt the drip of cream escaping her pussy, and that only served to heighten the desire pumping through her. Good god, she couldn't believe she was bent over like a naughty schoolgirl with everyone observing her aroused sex.

"The pelvic muscles are among the most important in our bodies," Jasen continued. "We use them for our posture, movement, and comfort. As a result, chronic tension builds. One way to relax those stressed muscles is by massage, or in our case, spanking becomes an effective form of massage. With each spank, we send heat and waves rippling through the muscle and those ripples bounce off bones. In turn, that stimulates the genitals. Blood floods the pelvis area, and all those delicious and sensitive the nerve endings flare to life, making sex intense, vivid, and arousing. Our queen will continue with the demonstration."

Smack!

The sharp slap and flash of fire startled Jessica who'd lost herself in the sexy drone of Jasen's voice. She let out a cry of shock that quickly morphed to a moan as a low hum vibrated deep in her center. The sting on her already sore and sensitive ass stroked nerve endings.

"Please note, when our queen spanked Rapunzel, she came up from beneath, an upswing. If you want to taunt your sub, raise your hand high, but come down and swing up, using a slightly cupped palm with fingers together. This method makes a pleasant smacking sound and reddens the skin gloriously without causing excessive pain. After you warm your sub's ass, if you deem she can take or wants more of the stinging pain, you can use a flat palm with spread fingers. I guarantee your partner will squirm and quiver with pleasure."

Smack! Smack! Smack!

The blows given with the flat of Glorie's hand, each spaced out, had Jessica crying out. Tears dripped onto the floor as the sting across her ass seeped deeper, the warmth spreading to encompass her sex and her entire middle that fluttered and clenched with a desperate desire for so much more.

Damn, she wanted to be fucked, and right now. She tried to clench her folds around her clit, but her feet were spread too far apart. She thought of Jasen, bringing the image of his red, swollen, and shiny cock to mind. Knowing he was turned on left her hungry for him to fuck her.

"My princess is sporting a pretty pink ass. Each spank adds to her growing tension. Take your time. Pause between to touch that lovely ass and enjoy the sight of your handprints covering her bottom. And subs, if you don't know when the next blow will fall, it adds tension, which increases your arousal. Doms, remember, it's not how many times you spank her or how hard that brings her into a high state of sexual readiness. It's how long, how deeply she feels, combined with her submissive helplessness."

Glorie trailed her nails along Jessica's shoulders. "Do you feel helpless, Rapunzel?"

Jessica moaned. "Yes, Mistress."

"Are you turned on?"

Good grief. She had to ask? Her clit was on fire, and she ached and throbbed deep inside. "Yes, Mistress."

The Domme slipped her finger inside Jessica's pussy. Jessica's eyes flashed wide, and she yelped in shock. Her cry dropped into a low moan when Glorie stroked in and out, then added a second finger. God, everyone was watching, seeing her juices drip, and that sent a fresh wave of moisture gushing to coat the Domme's fingers and make sucking noises.

Jessica finally admitted to herself that it thrilled her to know she was the center of attention. It no longer mattered who else was privy to something so private, only that she got what she needed and, in turn, gave others pleasure. This show wasn't just for her. At first, she'd felt alone and on display. Now, listening to the muffled sounds of pleasure and a higher squeak that proved someone had just enjoyed an orgasm, she realized she was as much a part of their intimacy as they were hers.

Glorie chuckled. "Yes, you are enjoying this." She eased her other hand beneath Jessica, touched her clit, and pinched her lips, trapping her clit between her folds.

Jessica tried to hold back a shriek of pleasure edging toward tormenting pain. Jasen continued to instruct, his voice thicker, deeper, as though he was having a hard time speaking.

"Doms, you want to alternate spanks with rubbing your sub's ass, using firm strokes to spread the warmth all over. Dip your finger into her crease and tease her anus, or better yet, engage in some back door play. Don't forget to test her pussy to see how wet and ready your sub is becoming. And as our queen is doing, tease her clit or tug her labia. This associates spanking with other pleasurable sensations and conditions your partner to being aroused during spanking. Take your time, savor every smack of that delectable behind."

Jessica panted, tensed with the burning desire to come, but the Domme removed both hands and resumed her demonstration, returning to the paddle and flogger, applying four spanks each. Jessica whimpered and couldn't stop crying. Her ass burned and stung, and her clit throbbed painfully, sending waves of pulsing need deep into her pussy. So many sensations, each one growing stronger, and helpless to do anything about any of them, she shook, quivered, and wept.

Spanking always left her with mixed emotions. She liked how it felt, and no doubt about it, her orgasms were bigger, deeper, and totally consumed her, but she also hated the fact that she felt helpless or that the pain made her cry like a baby.

She tried to muffle her cries when the whip once again struck. It produced sharper, tighter lines of pain where the paddle spread the sting over a wider area and the flogger bit into many areas at once. But she had to admit, she preferred the personal touch of the hand, which Glorie finished with, adding another four smacks in quick succession while that devious other hand snaked beneath her and pinched her clit.

Lost in a blur of emotion, pain, and desperate need, Jessica felt as though she'd been launched into a shockingly cold, clear world. Everything rushed together then exploded, sending her head over heels as her orgasm took hold with the tenacity of a bulldog with a bone.

Everything went numb and silent but for the racking spasms and pulses zinging through her clit and pussy. She jerked and spasmed out of control. She shrieked over and over, her cry of utter pleasure turning to a wail of protest when Glorie released her and dropped her down well before she was done.

Shaking and trembling, the pain rolling through her, she felt cheated. God, that orgasm could have gone on forever, she realized as aftershocks continued to roll through her.

Glorie's voice rang clear. "Doms, feel free to spank your subs."

The room filled with the sounds of flesh being spanked, sharp cries, and low moans.

"You did very well, little sub," the Domme said as she came around and knelt in front of Jessica, lifting her head with a finger to her chin, then removing her soaked mask. "You deserve a reward."

"You didn't let me finish." Jessica felt like crying with a different pain.

"No, I didn't. What else did I say I would do to you?"

Jessica sniffed. "Someday you'd fuck me."

God, was Glorie really going to fuck her? She'd taken her to a mind-numbing orgasm, but it hadn't been enough.

The Domme smiled gently. "And so I shall." She lowered her voice, used her thumbs to dry her face. "Tell me, Jessica. Do you want me to fuck you?"

She blinked, unsure, remembering that Jasen said he'd push her, that she wouldn't be bored, and the whole point of the weekend was to experience and explore her own sexuality. Someday she might want to be Glorie's sub, but right now, she wanted Jasen, craved his touch, his loving.

The Domme laughed softly. "A different time and place, I'd wear a strap on and fuck you until you scream, but alas, tonight is for you and your Dom, though I hope you enjoyed having part of your fantasy come true. The rest will have to wait I'm afraid."

She stood and moved away, leaving Jessica gasping at the image of the Domme literally fucking her. Her pussy wept, begged for his cock to enter and drive her wild, and Jessica prayed Jasen would come and take care of her and not make her wait until they returned to their tower room.

When Glorie motioned him forward, Jasen growled low in his throat and moved behind his sub, eager to finish the demonstration. His aching cock dripped with need, and he feared he might come right there. Jessica's ass bloomed with red roses on either cheek. The urge to fill his sub's pussy with his throbbing cock was hard to resist.

The entire demonstration had been sheer torture, and though his sub had cried and whimpered, tempting him to go to her and wipe her tears, he also admitted that from the way she wiggled her ass, panted, and gasped, she enjoyed having her fantasy realized. *Fuck it.* Glorie had that right.

He eyed her leaking cream, got onto his knees, and licked and swirled his tongue around and into her slit. The sounds of spanking from the audience faded beneath the pounding of blood in his ears. Jessica lifted her hips, inviting him to drink deep. Watching Glorie spank her and tease her pussy and clit had been sheer torture. Jessica's orgasm had been like a fist to his gut, and he swore his balls were twisted and tangled inside his too tight sac. Now, it was his turn. His mind was nearly numb with anticipation, his body on fire.

Chills raced down his spine, warning he was in danger of shooting a stream of cum into the condom he'd put on before coming on stage.

Standing, he plunged his dick into Jessica's swollen pussy. Their cries mingled as each had what they most desired.

She surrounded him with pure ecstasy. Her hot, swollen cunt convulsed as her body continued to spasm with her orgasm. Her pussy was alive and hungry and gripped his cock. He bucked forward, driven into a mindless frenzy as he pumped hard and fast. "Stay with me, princess."

On the verge, he let out a long, low groan as he fucked her like a man who'd been celibate for ten years. Her moans and cries spurred him on as did each explosion inside her swollen sheath as he sent her back up, kept her bucking and convulsing. His palms covered her reddened cheeks, parted her, allowing him to watch his cock drive in and out.

A sharp thwack to his backside tore a cry from his lips. He swung his head around and caught Glorie's pleased grin. Instead of protesting the unplanned paddling, he moaned. A second and third followed. He'd been about to come, but unbelievably, the pain shot him higher. Each time he yanked out, he presented his ass to Glorie who obliged him by smacking him hard enough to have him yelling. Each smack sent his cock arrowing back into Jessica's pussy.

Jessica screamed his name, and one last whack was all it took for him to take his encore bow with the biggest orgasm he'd ever experienced.

Chapter Eight

Early Friday morning, Jasen carried his mug of coffee to a small table on the far side of the tower, away from where Jessica slept. Day one of the fairy tale event had not only wiped her out, but he felt fucked out as well. He let out a low moan as he took his first sip of hot caffeine. Hazelnut, his favorite.

As he waited for the jolt to hit his system, he set up his laptop, hating to dig into work, but an SOS text from his sister warned that things were not going good at the office. He sat, then popped up with a wince, barely managing to bite back the yell that punched from rear to throat. He rubbed his ass. Damn, Glorie's paddling last night had left him tender. That made him smile.

The brief flare of pain was a nice reminder of an awesome event. He settled gingerly. The demonstrations planned by Bryce and Glorie, the two in charge of the entire weekend, far surpassed anything he could have come up with on his own, and while each show was hot, he had to admit, his and Jessica's had to top the hot list. Though Goldie and her Bears had been hot enough to melt steel. The two Doms and two subs put on a very arousing show of multiple players and double penetration.

He shook his head. Well, Alice earned points for her willingness to demo various toys and bondage. He hoped to try some of those toys out on Jessica later, and shit, if he was being fair, the anal demonstration got them all hot and eager for more. He glanced up into the loft tucked above and chuckled. The thought of recreating that scene was top on his list for tonight. Yeah, he had plans for them.

Scrolling through his messages, he found several from his sister. As he read, his good cheer evaporated.

"Shit." Not only did he not have a place to hold the event, he no longer had an event director. What else could go wrong? He fired off a couple replies, pulled up his files, and got to work.

****

Jessica woke with a grin and a groan. She was so stiff, she could barely move. Blinking against the bright light, she rolled onto her back. Oh god, her poor ass was more than a bit sore. Despite the pain, she smiled happily. Last night had been one of the most fantastic evenings she'd ever experienced.

Who knew she was such an exhibitionist? Or that she'd get such a thrill out of starring in her own scene, but the cherry on her sundae had been having a woman fuck her. Good god, that had been mind-boggling.

She rolled to the side so she could study Jasen while he slept. She frowned when she realized she was alone in the king-sized bed. Sitting carefully, she glanced around the room and spotted him on the far side, working. His hair stood on end as though he'd been running his hands through it. Her brows rose. She slid out of bed and grabbed her silky robe from the floor. "I thought all electronic devices were banned. She'd been forced to leave her phone with Hastings. No phones, tablets, or computers."

Jasen tore his attention from his laptop. "You're awake."

"You're up. I didn't mean to sleep so late." She left the bed and joined him at the table.

"You needed it, princess. And more than earned it." He rose. "Coffee?"

"Yes, please. Whatever you have. Smells heavenly. Black. What's the plan for today?"

Jasen set a mug in front of her. "We rest. We can walk in the woods or go down to the garden. You had quite a day yesterday."

She grinned. "I wouldn't change a thing, either." She pointed to his laptop and the papers he was gathering. "What's all that?"

"Just some work stuff. I'll put it away. I apologize. I shouldn't have gotten it out. I broke the rules. You can spank me if you wish."

Though he said the words lightly and with an apologetic grin, the smile didn't reach his clouded green eyes. "I think I'll leave the spanking to Glorie."

He groaned. "I'd forgotten how good our queen is with a paddle."

Jessica lifted one brow. "She's spanked you before?"

He nodded. "In college. She and I were lovers for a while, and once I discovered that I was happier being the top, she tutored me in all areas of sex and BDSM. And how about you? Did your fantasy live up to your expectations?"

Just thinking about her fantasy playing out and Glorie's expert ministrations sent a wave of heat up her neck and into her cheeks. "Oh my god, I never expected that." Glorie hadn't just spanked her. She'd fucked her with her fingers, and Jessica had come. Her cheeks burned when she recalled the queen's promise for more. "You blush so nicely, princess. I could tell you liked it."

She shook her head. "Loved it." She wrinkled her nose. "That doesn't upset you, does it? After all, I'm your sub, not hers." She took a nervous sip of coffee.

Jasen wrapped his hand in her long, tousled blonde hair and tugged gently until his lips met hers in a sweet, brushing kiss. "Did you enjoy the evening, Jessica?"

"You know I did. You said I wouldn't be bored, and you were so right." She'd never had such an intense few hours in her life. The anal demonstration had been hot, and the spanking, along with being fucked by both Glorie and Jasen had nearly done her in. She'd barely been able to rouse herself by the time Goldie and her three bears had taken front and center.

"As your Dom, it is my responsibility to help you discover your sexuality and that means trying new things. You were so damn hot. I almost humiliated myself and came right there on the floor." Another sweep of his mouth across her lips had her sighing.

"We didn't try out the rest of the toys."

After carrying her back to their play area, Jasen had taken care of her sore ass. Spent emotionally and physically, he'd held her close. She'd enjoyed the next show that followed but hadn't managed even a small orgasmic pop to join in the audience participation.

And that was too bad as there were a couple of toys she wouldn't have minded him using on her, especially if he employed a few of the bondage techniques used on Alice. Goldie's show? That had revived both her and Jasen. Talk about hot. No half-hearted pops there, more like a nuclear blast that mushroomed them both into the stratosphere.

But what she'd really enjoyed was the way he'd held her during the night, pulling her against him, cradling her close as though she were special. She seldom spent an entire night with a Dom, preferring to return to her own place and avoid those awkward mornings after. A small smile tugged her lips upward. All that holding had led to a couple of slow, lazy sessions of loving in the early morning. She found she liked that tender, gentle side of Jasen.

"We have the rest of the weekend." He forced a laugh and started gathering his scattered outlines and notes.

Curious, she reached out and stopped him from clearing the table. "Talk to me, Jasen. Talk to me like I'm an intelligent woman. Don't treat me like an empty headed blonde or a silly little girl who needn't worry her *silly little head* about something she can't possibly understand."

He froze. "I didn't mean to imply—Jessica—"

"Then tell me what's wrong. It doesn't matter if I understand or not. Just treat me like an equal, like you used to. Don't pander or placate me."

"Okay." He brushed the hair from her face. "I truly wasn't trying to belittle you, princess." He leaned back. "You know I run a children's charity, with the goal of recruiting foster homes and training couples to be better parents. I don't want to attract those only looking for the money the state pays. My goal is to create stable families and stop the bouncing. Even encourage adoption when it's feasible. I want homes like the one I had with the McPherson's. They didn't care about the money and always made sure we had everything we needed. So many pocket the money or spend it on other things without even giving the children they take in decent clothes or shoes."

He ran a hand through his hair. "Our latest success is with a gay couple who've taken in two teens who were kicked out of their homes for being gay. Not many families are willing to take on a child who is different. They are already talking about adopting the boys, making a real family." He shrugged. "That is what I really want—permanent homes, permanent families.

Once again, she felt a stab of jealousy that he had such selfless goals. "I like that. You're doing something good for society. So what's the problem?"

"Our main fundraiser is now on hold."

"What happened?" She drank her coffee and kept her gaze on Jasen. She couldn't remember ever having a conversation with any of her other lovers that wasn't centered on sex or polite small talk the next morning.

"We were set for a formal dinner and auction. We lost the hotel. They decided to remodel. And with time short—"

"How short?"

"Less than three months."

She set her cup down with a thump. "Jasen! You won't find another hotel in time. Not in San Francisco or any of the surrounding cities. The big ones book a year out."

He tipped his cup to her. "That was my first problem. And now my event director has quit. Run off to Reno with her boyfriend where they plan to live." He shut his laptop with a snap. "Not much to do until Monday."

Jessica riffled through the papers, scanning budgets, and forecasts, projects in the works, future goals, mission statements, and an outline for the event. "You don't have time to lose. Let's work on it for a while. Tell me more about your event. I might be able to make some suggestions."

"It's not your problem, princess."

Her gaze shot to his. He glanced away. "You don't think I can help you with this? Poor Jessica only knows how to party and shop." Bitterness laced her words.

Jasen wanted to curse himself for putting that sad, haunted look back on her face. *Shit.* "I didn't say that. At this point, I probably have to cancel." God, he hated the thought of canceling, but right now, he wasn't sure he could pull it together.

"If we are taking today to rest up, why not work on this? You're worried, and I might be able to help. I've worked on lots of charities and fundraisers. There's no reason we can't take at least part of the day to go over your options."

He didn't want to insult her or hurt her feelings, but what he required was an experienced event planner. He had no doubt she did her share of charity and fundraisers, but he'd bet she worked the events themselves, not the behind the scenes stuff that could be hard and grueling. "Look, Jessica—"

She jumped from her chair and leaned forward, palms flat on the table. "Jasen McPherson, you think I'm worthless."

Seeing true distress mingling with fury in her eyes, Jasen caved. How he'd stood up to her in high school, he had no idea. That hurt little girl look, the sheen of tears, turned his mind to mush. "You don't have to prove anything to me, princess."

"What if I want to prove something to myself," she said softly, a single tear escaping to trail down her silky, soft cheek.

Just like that, Jasen was a goner. That freight train chasing him since the night he'd chosen her to be his partner flattened him on the tracks.

****

"Okay, explain to me who your targeted sponsors are." Jessica was reading the invitation list, seeing several politicians, business leaders, the mayor, as well as Bryce and Glorie. She also recognized a few names of those in her father's circle of friends, but the rest of the nearly two hundred guests, she had no idea of their status or wealth. As she knew many of the movers and shakers, she wanted to see if he was targeting those who were a match for his charity.

Jasen lay on his side on a quilt spread out beneath the trees. It was afternoon, the air warm, the breeze refreshing. Dappled sunlight spilled from the canopy of leaves above them. She shifted slightly to avoid a spear of light to her eyes.

"We target those we think might be receptive to helping children, and those with fat wallets. This is our yearly fundraiser. Some of the guests are those who are donating items to the auction and the raffle."

She nodded, chewed the cap of her pen, and then shook her head. "I don't see how we're going to find a place to accommodate this many people in so short a time." She glanced at Jasen, noticed he was watching her and not listing his resources for her. She asked about his connections, who they could call upon to give time, money, or other resources, like hotel managers. A list of her and her father's network of friends and associates in the business community lay between them. A star marked those she believed might prove useful. Too bad, she didn't have her phone. She could start making calls.

Tapping her nails on the table, she frowned. Something was bothering her, but what? With exception of finding a new venue, she could find no fault with the event itself. For a moment, she let her doubts creep in. What had she been thinking? She'd never organized an event on this scale, but she'd been around those who did all her life.

Again, none of those people had asked her to do any real work or planning, including her father. She was nothing more than a pretty face and the daughter of a wealthy man no one wanted to offend. But that didn't mean she hadn't observed and smirked when she noticed mistakes being made. Mentally, she shrugged. Twice she'd tried to point out flaws or holes in plans, and both times, she'd been patted on the head, brushed off, or given some pointless task. She'd learned to keep her mouth shut.

Tapping her finger, she sighed. "Something is nagging me." She tossed the folder to the quilt.

"Take a break. I told you we wouldn't be able to do much here."

"I guess." She glanced at Jasen. God, it was so hard to reconcile her nerdy lab partner with her Dom. Right now, he was just a man. A very relaxed, good-looking man. As he'd said earlier, today was their day of rest. She adjusted the pillow beneath her. Her bum was still sore, and seeing him stretched out, she figured his was as well.

"This is nice." He'd kept to his word, and they'd spent the day working on his event and enjoying each other's company. Trouble was, the more she looked, the more she wanted to touch, and if she touched, she'd want to take, but he'd made no move to resume their roles of Dom and sub.

"We're not done for the weekend, are we?"

He laughed. "You can't want more?"

She flushed. "I'm not sure I could ever get too much of you, Sir." And wasn't that the truth? Seldom did she ever use a Dom more than a few times at most. She was always searching for better. With Jasen, she'd found the best. He made her body sing, and he challenged her as well. He didn't bore her.

Her gaze swept over him. He wore a simple tunic and pants, and she was once again in a dress much like the one she'd worn the first night. In school, she'd hated the boy he'd been. He'd angered and frustrated her, and looking back, she admitted that perhaps that hate had been something else. He'd made it clear she was the last girl on earth he'd have anything to do with outside of schoolwork so she'd turned those budding feelings of like or infatuation to anger and hate.

And now? Those long hidden desires were growing, leaving the dark corner of her heart where she'd buried them. Trouble was, he still didn't view her as a woman worth taking on beyond a weekend of pleasure.

"Why the frown, princess?"

She shook off the encroaching depression. Once the weekend was over, he probably wouldn't see her again. Unless—

"You're right in that we can't do much while we are here. I want to work on this next week." No, she wanted more than that. She needed to prove to herself—and to him—that there was more to her than parties, fun times, and endless shopping trips. She felt trapped, locked in a gilded cage. Something deep inside her yearned to break free.

"Jessica, you don't have to do this."

She drew her knees up, not even caring that she wore no panties. For the first time in her life, she wasn't trying to get her way by using her sexuality. "Yes, I do. Hire me, Jasen. Hire me as Event Director."

His brows shot up. "That's a far cry from helping me this weekend, princess. There's a lot more to the job than this fundraiser. It's a full time position."

"I can learn. Starting with this event. Let me take charge and make this happen. If I succeed, we talk about you hiring me permanently. If not..." She shrugged, determined to make sure it was successful.

"I don't know, Jessica—"

This was too important, a turning point in her life and maybe what she'd been trying to find for so many years. "You're the one who said I don't have ambitions, dreams, or goals. No accomplishments. You asked if there was more than parties for Jessica Lowe and said I needed to earn my way. Was that all fancy shrink talk? Did you or did you not mean those words?"

Jasen flopped onto his back. "Yes, I meant them." *Chug-chug-chug. Here comes that fucking train again.*

"Then give me this, Jasen. Don't be like my father or everyone else who think I'm a dumb blonde."

Thump. Once again, he was slammed, but instead of being flattened like roadkill, that iron monster swept him up, tossed him against the pilot, the front end of the engine, as they shot down the tracks with him plastered to the train with nothing to hold onto. He could only hope the runaway train didn't stop suddenly and fling him to hell and back because, for better or worse, he wanted this woman in his life.

"All right, princess. This event only, and then we'll evaluate. And we work together, just like in high school. Be warned, if I don't like your work, I'll make you do it over."

Jessica threw herself on top of him. "Thank you, Jasen. You won't be sorry. If you aren't too worn out, I think there is a way I can show my appreciation right now." Her eyes gleamed with lust.

He threaded his hands in her hair, the silky softness making him groan even as a wide smile formed. "Good god, woman, you can't be serious."

With a wide grin, she stood, pulled her dress over her head, knelt, and ran her hand over his growing bulge. "With your permission, Sir, I believe your cock would like to come out to play."

"Maybe—" He sucked in his breath. As in the elevator, she had his pants open and his cock out before he finished speaking. "We need to do something about your habit of rushing things, princess."

Her fist closed over him. He eyed the curve of her back as she bent over to lick his dick, her ass high, teasing him with glimpses of her pretty, pink flesh.

"On me," he ordered, urging her to straddle his body in the classic sixty-nine position. Hot needles swarmed his blood, sticking and stabbing, sending tingles from the top of his head to his toes when she licked his rod from root to tip.

"Playing with fire, princess." Jasen groaned and wrapped his hands around her hips, holding her close. His nostrils flared as he breathed deeply, drawing in her aroused musk. Sparks of excitement, like those from a popping campfire rose from his cock and exploded in his head, short circuiting thoughts and reason.

"Not playing," she panted. "Taking."

God, was there anything he wanted more than to be taken by this woman? All his worries fell away. There was only him, his princess, and today. She continued to lick his dick. Laying the flat of his tongue against her, he lapped her juices from slit to clit, his tongue cleaving through her swollen folds. Her taste exploded in his mouth and shot into his dick. She jerked, moaned, and scrapped her teeth across the head of his cock before dipping the tip of her exploring tongue into the weeping slit to drink from him. He retaliated by plunging his tongue deep inside her cunt.

"Good idea," he gasped when she challenged him by swirling around his swollen head, flicking the tender skin beneath, and again, paying attention to his seeping tip. He reciprocated by mirroring her movements, teasing and taunting her swelling nub and thrusting deep inside her pussy.

She let out a cry. "Damn good. I'm better." She swallowed his cock, sucking him deep.

"Fuck!" His head arched back. His dick vibrated with the urge to come, and his balls tightened painfully. She set a brutal pace.

Unwilling to be outdone or leave her behind, he closed his lips around her clit and sucked that tiny nub deep, matching her rhythm, giving her tit for tat. What started out as a thank you and show of appreciation turned into a battle of wills. Or tongues.

Jessica sucked Jasen's cock long, hard, and deep. She opened her throat and squeezed his soft, fleshy crown. His rumbling groan shot up through her clit like a vibrator. She threw her head back to release the cry clawing its way free. Gasping, she stared at his glistening, pulsing rod pushing up from her fist, reminding her of crystals in a cave stretching from floor to ceiling.

"Shiny." She moaned as he worked her, sucking and laving until she shivered and trembled. How easy it would be to stop what she was doing and let him drive her over the edge. Her nipples dangled and rubbed against the rasp of hair that ran down his belly like an arrow pointing the way to great pleasures. Electrical pulses zipped from her tips to her clit trapped between his lips and fizzled deep inside her like sparklers on the Fourth of July.

Drawing in a deep breath, she closed her mouth over his cock, unwilling to lose focus or be outdone. She'd wanted to please him, but holy cow, he was pleasing the hell out of her. She found it incredibly erotic to have him mirroring her actions. With one hand holding him by the root, she eased her other fingers between his legs and grabbed his hard, tight balls, pulling them gently away from his body, allowing her to squeeze and play with his twin toys.

"Fuck-fuck-fuck."

She grinned around her mouthful even as her clit cried out against the loss of his mouth. Determined to make her Dom, her new boss, and maybe, just maybe her friend come before her, she slicked her finger with her spit, bobbed her head up and down, harder and faster, and with both hands free, she parted his cheeks. Before he knew what she was about, she fingered the tight ring of convulsing muscle, pressing the pad of her wet finger to that tight rosebud, teasing him with her nail. He bucked, sending his huge cock sliding down her open throat. He growled and moaned low and long. The sounds hummed through her, shoving her ever closer to the edge and the temptation to throw out her hands and just fly.

"Fire—princess," he panted. "Might get—burned."

"Being a good sub. Taking care of my Dom." God, she was close to coming. She sucked harder, eased her finger in farther, and with her other hand, pressed on the spot between anus and his tight sac. At the same time, he shoved two fingers into her pussy.

Mouths to clit and cock, fingers to pussy and ass became sweet torture for both Dom and sub. Jessica held off her climax until Jasen shouted and a hot stream of cum jettisoned down her throat, leaving a musky, salty taste in her mouth.

Still shouting her name, he got his revenge by pressing hard against that dime-size rough patch inside her that shot her over the edge. Her shriek joined his roar. And high above them, their shouts startled a flock of blackbirds who took to the air with cries of their own.

Chapter Nine

Wearing a gown in deep rose, Jessica got in line at the top of the stairs the night of the ball. She'd spent the afternoon with Alice getting her hair done, nails polished, enjoying massages, and all the girly things she did regularly without thinking anything about it while the other woman had oohed and ahhed, telling her the spa day was a treat.

She admired the women dressed in their finery. Cinderella in blue, Red Riding Hood in red and black, Wendy in a shimmering gown of a palest pink bodice with layers of pale green tulle over a pink skirt, Belle in deep blue, and Alice in a sleek column of burnt orange. The evil fairy wore black of course.

A week ago, she'd have been all about who wore what from what designer, but aside from admiring each woman in her gown, her mind was otherwise engaged. She had a job. Her very first job. God, she was giddy with happiness, yet paralyzed with fear.

She plucked at the silky fabric of her skirt. What if she failed? What if her father was right, that she should just stick to her little charities where no one expected anything from her and in return, she'd feel no sense of accomplishment? No, she could do this—would do this. Too much was at stake, and not just for the children. She wanted above all else to make Jasen proud and earn his praise. And maybe more. If there was one thing she was good at, it was reading people, and she knew he was interested in her.

In her.

The words sent a thrill down her spine. She couldn't remember anyone being interested in Jessica Lowe, the person. Jessica, the wealthy socialite, yes. Jessica, the sexy bombshell, yup. Jessica, daughter of billionaire Roland Lowe. But interested in just her, stripped of all trappings? No one.

As Jasen said, it was sad, but sadder still was the truth that she'd done it to herself. She'd passively accepted those confining labels and taken the easy way out and acted accordingly.

When she reached the top of the stairs, glanced down, and spotted her prince in a deep burgundy tunic and black slacks waiting for her, she vowed to break free of the molds life had forced her to adopt and become who she wanted to be. From now on, she'd make a difference. And hope that Jasen saw beyond their past. She wasn't hoping for a future. Not yet. Just today. And tomorrow would turn into another today.

When Hastings boomed out her character's name, she took the stairs one at a time. Just like she'd take the rest of her life—one day at a time.

After hours of dancing, nibbling on finger foods and more turns across the gleaming dance floor, Jessica escaped to the powder room. She sat at a vanity to freshen her make up. Bo and Mary bustled in with Bo talking a mile a minute, finding fault with something or the other. Jessica wrinkled her nose. She didn't like Jeri. The woman was a mean gossip at the clubs.

Jessica stared at her reflection and wasn't sure she knew that woman any more.

Or maybe she no longer wanted to be the woman she'd been a few days ago. Yes, that was it. For the first time in her life, she wanted more for herself, and money wasn't going to get it. She contemplated Jasen's charity. She admired him for devoting much of his free time to helping others. Even his job focused on helping children in difficult situations. He was an admirable, giving man.

And she, Jessica Lowe, was as self-centered as they came. Until now. She wasn't sure how to make such a drastic change. It wouldn't be easy, but she was quite determined to do this. And not just to impress Jasen. She wanted to do it for herself. Jasen had taught her that she was worth so much more.

No more boring parties or engaging in excesses to relieve her boredom. And if working for Jasen didn't work out? Well, she'd find something, but right now, she had a job to do, and to get it done would take a miracle. Good grief. They had less than three months to pull together a fundraising event. For a moment, she worried her lower lip, ruining her freshly applied sheen of lip-gloss.

Thinking and fretting, she wondered if she'd bitten off more than she could live up to. She allowed the maid to fuss with her hair and tuck loose strands back in the fancy do. Another woman hurried in, but she didn't pay attention. In her mind, she was bringing up different venues. The bigger hotels were booked, as well as vineyards with facilities for a catered dinner. She had a list of places to call come Monday but didn't hold out any hope.

She sighed. On top of what seemed impossible, there was something bothering her about what Jasen had planned. By his own admission, they raised a decent amount of money each year, but they needed families, resources, homes, and volunteers. These charity events only targeted those with deep pockets, which then allowed him and his staff to work on their other needs using advertising and education.

But what if the event was broader, opened up to a more diverse group? Bring in prospective volunteers, foster parents, business leaders who didn't have the big bucks, but were willing to, in some way, contribute to the children of their community?

She smiled her thanks to the maid and stood.

Out in the hall, she ordered herself to put it away and focus on her time with Jasen. There was no point in getting ahead of herself by thinking bigger when, at this late date, they wouldn't even be able to book a picnic area at a park.

She froze as the word lit up in her mind and flashed like a neon sign. "How utterly simple. And brilliant," she whispered as she rushed back into the ballroom, her thoughts racing.

****

Jasen spotted Jessica threading her way around dancers. Her beauty and grace simply dazzled him.

She truly was a princess. In his hands, he had two flutes of champagne and waited for her to rejoin him near the terrace doors.

In his opinion, she outshone everyone in the bright ballroom. Whirling her across the gleaming dance floor, he'd felt like her prince, her one true love. When she stopped in front of him, her eyes sparkling behind her mask, he handed her a glass. "You're beautiful, princess."

And she was his princess. What started as a less than complimentary name had become so much more. No matter how many times during the evening he'd told himself it was only a weekend, that they came from two very different worlds, his heart insisted on wanting what it could never have.

"You're pretty princely yourself, Sir."

His hand cupped her behind her neck. "Jasen. Tonight we are equals."

He swore she vibrated with excitement. And why shouldn't she? She was born to shine at parties.

She smiled shyly. "I like that. Jasen." She leaned into him, lifted her mouth.

How could he resist? He brought her closer, kissed her gently, lightly, even though he wanted nothing more than to claim her with a kiss hard and deep enough to leave them both breathless.

To his surprise, she pulled back, took him by the arm, and led the way onto the terrace, finding a secluded corner. "Don't tell me you can't wait to get to the room?" He wasn't above doing some necking to warm things up. He had plans for that loft area tonight.

She rolled her eyes. "I am capable of thinking

of more than sex, Jasen."

"I'm sorry to hear it," he joked, smiling. "Sex with you is pretty damn hot."

She laughed. "Okay, I'll agree. It's good."

"Just good?" He brushed her mouth with his.

"Better than good as you well know." Again, she eased back.

Gripping her chin, he wished he could see her eyes clearly, but between the mask and the shadows, with only faint light from the lanterns strung around the patio, he only saw the glitter in their depths. Excitement or tears? "What's wrong, Jessica?"

"Nothing," she replied, her voice low and husky as though she were holding back.

"Be honest, princess."

She set her glass down. "This is a party and it's pretty fantastic and as lavish as they come, but would you be terribly disappointed if I wanted to leave and go back to our room?"

His flute joined hers. He cupped her face in his hands. "What's wrong?"

He'd noticed Jeri and her friend leaving, most likely to make use of the bathroom as well. The woman was trouble, so much so he'd banned her from his club as she couldn't keep confidences and was just a bitch besides. How it was that the senator who was one of her subs trusted her, he had no idea. The man was playing with fire with his political career.

So had Jeri said something to Jessica? She'd been a happy, regal princess all night, talking to others, dancing in his arms, and teasing him with the brush of her tits against his chest, her hip sliding across the cock. But what he saw and heard now wasn't sexual.

She threw her arms around his neck, hugging him. "Nothing's wrong. Everything is wonderful." She pulled back, grinning widely. "And I have the perfect solution to our event problems. I have a place."

He blinked, her words taking him by complete surprise. "Where?"

"First, the heart of all this is the children, correct?"

"Of course."

"Then you're going about this all wrong. You need to focus on the children. We're putting on a big ass picnic at my father's mansion." She grabbed him by the arm and led the way down the terrace, through the ballroom, and into the elevator.

This time, sex wasn't on his mind. In horror, he stared at the woman who was slowly stealing his heart. "A picnic?"

He followed her into their room, protesting. "Jessica, we need money and that means a formal event to draw the top tier of our community."

She ignored him and sat at the table, uncaring of her gown. "Wait. Let me outline what I have I mind."

He paced. How the hell had he been sucked in so completely? Realizing the weekend of fantasy had ended, he wondered just what he'd let himself in for. A picnic? He hated to disappoint her but it was out of the question. Better to cancel and reschedule.

When Jessica called him over and outlined her idea, shock and horror gave way to awe. Her plan was nothing short of brilliance. If she could pull it off.

****

Six weeks later, Jasen walked into his office, unsurprised to find Jessica sitting at an old, scarred, beaten-up metal desk. He'd offered to purchase a new desk, but she'd refused, said she'd work with what they had. He grimaced mentally. Everything in his office was beyond used, but he hadn't wanted to spend money on comfort and design if it meant taking it away from funds better spent bettering the lives of foster children. He *had* insisted on a new chair.

Leaning against the doorjamb, he watched her typing away on the computer, consulting a list, then a scrap of paper with more notes before resuming her data input.

Every morning, he arrived before the staff and even his sister, yet Jessica, most days, beat him into the office. The first few days he'd figured it was just something new, like a new toy, and soon enough, she'd wander in on her own time and eventually become bored with the repetitious work. Even the most devoted person on his staff grew tired or discouraged when told no to any of their requests for money, donations for the raffle, or pleas for volunteers.

But not Jessica. The more she was told no, the more determined she became. Jasen had to admit, she'd infused his organization with new enthusiasm. After all, if the rich girl could handle it, then so could everyone else.

His gaze swept over her. No one looking at her would know she had a wardrobe fit for a queen—or princess. She wore worn jeans, sneakers, and T-shirts just like everyone else. And with her pale hair pulled back into a ponytail, she looked young and carefree, nothing like the haughty sub who challenged all the club Doms. He shook his head, totally bemused and enchanted.

A picnic. A fairy tale picnic to boot!

Jasen was still amazed that she'd pounced on the heart of his charity and made it the focal point of his event. They were hosting a big ass barbecue at her father's mansion. The guest list included children and foster parents in his program as well as children needing placement. That was what Jessica called their center. Everyone and everything revolved around them.

He strode into the room and set a go-cup of coffee in front of her. "Coffee, princess?"

She glanced up. "Thanks, and you're not supposed to call me that here."

He grinned. "No one here but the two of us." He eased a hip onto her desk and grimaced when it rocked.

"And some of us have a ton of phone calls to make," she said primly. "Can't give my slave-driver of a boss an excuse to find fault. He's very exacting, you know." She eyed him, her blue eyes sparkling with mischief. "He's even been known to spank."

The sweet curve of her lips sent an arrow of lust deep into his gut. "Perhaps the boss might not mind it if his star worker stumbled a bit so he could catch her. Or just hold and comfort her." He pulled her up from her chair and with his hands on her ass and lifted her onto his thigh. "Might give him an excuse for some one-on-one instruction."

His mouth claimed hers, his tongue sweeping inside, tasting a hint of coffee, vanilla, and cream. Her arms swept around his neck, and her thighs tightened around his as he kissed her hard and deep until they were both breathless.

He lifted his head and stared into eyes that were soft and full of need. "Will you be naughty today, princess?"

She moaned. "We can't, Jasen. Not until after."

"But you want me." And he wanted her to the point of pain.

"Yes, Sir. I want you very much."

"Then have dinner with me. Tonight." He nuzzled her throat with his lips.

"We had dinner last night. And the night before. In fact, we've had dinner every night since leaving Pleasure Manor."

"Wrong, princess. We've missed three nights. Two you had plans with your father, and I had a family birthday dinner."

"Yeah, but you came over after." Her breathing turned shallow when he dug his fingers into her jean-encased ass and stroked her against his hard thigh.

"I want more than dinners with my princess. I want the appetizers, the meals, and deserts. Come home with me. Or let me stay the night at your place."

Jessica sighed. "I can't—we can't. I have to

prove to you, and myself, that I can do this. I want more from my life than parties and dating. I want to be useful. I want my life to have meaning."

Jasen sighed. "You have already proven yourself, Jessica. The job is yours."

"No. I won't take it until this event is over. I won't let you give it to me. I have to earn it, just like you made me earn my grades in high school." She feathered her fingers across his jawline. "I want to be more than the woman you have sex with and dinners with. I want to prove I can do this, and if we spend the night together, we won't sleep—

Jasen nabbed one hand and nipped her fingers. "True. I can think of many things I want to do with you besides sleeping."

"Behave. I want to give this job my best. It's too important—to you, to me, and to the children. Besides, I don't want everyone thinking I got the job because I'm sleeping with the boss."

Shaking his head ruefully, Jasen leaned close and rubbed his forehead against hers. "Yet you got the job because you *were* sleeping with the boss." His palms glided up beneath her tee, his fingers tracing the curve of her spine.

She pulled back and sighed. "I want to do this my way. I want to prove I can do this."

He smiled. "You are doing this, Jessica. I cannot believe how much you've done or the scope of this event. It's bigger than anything we've ever put on."

A spear of heat arrowed into her heart. Jasen's words ignited a glow deep inside that had nothing to do with his kiss and heated embrace. She shifted away, feeling the loss of his heat and the comfort of his arms keenly. "Maybe too big? Too much?"

Those destructive doubts crept in like a prowling panther waiting for just the right moment to pounce. So much rested upon her success—their success.

Jasen stood, rested his hands on her shoulders. "We'll do this your way, but when this is over, we're going to discuss this no sleeping with the boss rule." He bent his head and kissed her hungrily.

When he lifted his head, Jessica was more than tempted to beg for more. She couldn't remember the last time she'd deliberately denied herself sex. Hell, she'd never in her entire life denied herself anything she really wanted.

He tipped her chin and stared into her eyes. "Dinner tonight. Don't argue with the boss." He deepened his voice.

The sub inside her nearly melted at his feet. The gleam in his eyes warned that he'd used his demanding voice deliberately.

"Yes, Sir," she said softly, her gaze following him as he strode to his desk. She resumed her seat and stared blankly at her screen. Her stomach was in flutters. It hurt to turn him down, turn him away, when everything inside her demanded she take what he so freely offered, what she so desperately needed.

Every moment spent with him, whether in the office or in the evenings during dinners or long drives or strolling through the Golden Gate Park during lunch, deepened her feelings for him. Taking a deep breath, she admitted she'd fallen in love with Jasen and wanted him, and his love, more than she'd ever wanted anything in the world.

But it had to be as equals—except for in the bedroom. There she wanted her Dom. Once she'd been content to just take. But no longer. She didn't want to be the little rich girl who slid through life on her good looks and her daddy's fortune and name. She didn't want the endless stream of parties and traveling.

Most of all, she didn't want a pity job. Her money, status, and social position in the community meant nothing to Jasen, but it mattered to her. God, she yearned to be recognized for herself, for her own actions and deeds. He'd pushed her in high school, expected her to rise to her full potential, and though she knew he didn't expect a miracle from her now, she wanted to give it to him.

So much was riding against them. Time was short, the workload overwhelming. But she could do it, had to do it, had to make sure this event was a success, and she absolutely had to prove to Jasen that, like in high school, there was more to her than a pretty face and a sexy body. Only then could she talk about a future.

If she failed? She shrugged mentally. If she failed, she wouldn't have anything to offer Jasen because she wouldn't have anything left inside her to give.

****

Jasen wanted nothing more than to sweep Jessica into his arms and carry her away someplace where it was just the two of them as it had been at

Pleasure Manor, but he understood her reasoning, even if he didn't agree with it. She'd told him she wanted to focus on the job at hand without the distraction of sex, but he knew that wasn't the whole truth.

She was distancing herself, keeping him at arm's length in case she failed. She hadn't put it into words, but he knew if she failed, he'd lose her. Worse, he feared she'd lose herself. No matter how many times he told her they were in this pickle together, that they succeeded together or failed together, it didn't matter. She'd accepted his challenge and the responsibility, even though it wasn't all hers to shoulder.

What would he do if she walked away? No one watching her work, listening to her on the phone, could find fault or accuse her of slacking off or not doing her best. But that wasn't enough for her. He knew it was all or nothing. If they succeeded, he had a chance. If not, he'd lose the only woman who'd ever touched his heart.

****

The days blurred into weeks and weeks morphed into months until they were down to the wire with only two weeks to go. Stress levels climbed and worry churned in his gut like waves crashing on the shore. He worked long hours, often staying up half the night. Fuck, he couldn't sleep anyway, couldn't eat, and couldn't concentrate. During the day, he had his work and his passion. At night, he took to bed with him his fear, instead of the woman he loved.

On the phone, listening to canned music while

on hold, he glanced up when he heard Jessica's triumphant shout. She jumped to her feet and did her happy dance all the way across the room to a freestanding white board. A blown up map of her father's estate filled one entire side. Small squares of bright colors indicated different activity areas. He hung up and crossed off another item on his list that grew daily.

Standing, he joined her as she pinned a name to the activity labeled water dunk. His jaw dropped. "You got the mayor and the police commissioner to agree to be dunked?"

Grinning, she pointed her fingers to the ceiling and danced. "Who's the man?" she chanted.

He shook his head. "I've been trying to get the mayor to one of these events for years. How'd you convince him?"

"Easy. Mayor said he'd do it if the commissioner did. He didn't know the commissioner is a personal friend of my father's." She wagged her brows. "Or the fact that he's also my godfather."

"Amazing." He pulled her into his arms, and because they were alone in the office, he kissed her. "We're just about there."

Jessica gave him a hard kiss back then wiggled free. "No distracting me. I'm on a roll. Go finish your list. Time's running short."

"You're a hard taskmaster, princess." He grinned. The mayor and the commissioner. He returned to his desk and couldn't help watching the woman he loved. He'd never thought that boyhood infatuation could grow and consume him.

To say she was driven was an understatement. She'd taken to this task like white to rice, and he couldn't believe how much she'd accomplished in so little time. Seemed money greased more than wheels. She had people falling all over her to take part in what was being called one of the biggest events of the year. No one dared tell her no. He couldn't count the number of times she'd dropped her father's name or reminded someone how much he'd contributed to his or her charity or political fundraisers.

He'd called her on it, but she'd shrugged and asked what good was wealth and status if you couldn't use it for good, and the children were worth the favors she'd owe in return. He stared at the pile of checks his sister had dumped on his desk that morning that were waiting for him to log and bank.

Saying no to Jessica tended to cost a pretty penny. He glanced at the clock. It was well past quitting time, but as he'd learned, when she was on a roll, he had to threaten to put her over his shoulder and carry her out.

He shook his head. How life had changed since that night at the club when he'd cemented his future by putting her name forward as his partner and as his princess.

The train that had threatened to flatten him had instead taken him on one hell of an adventure. With only two weeks to go, he returned to his list, making sure the rental equipment they needed would be there on time. They were down to the final hurdles, rounding that bend to the finish line, and his life felt like that hush before the crowd went wild. Trouble was, there was still so much work to be done and organized that he wasn't sure if that collective crowd would cheer or moan.

Chapter Ten

The day of the picnic was fairy tale perfect. Her father's expansive grounds transformed into a mini theme park. Jump houses and slides themed around a princess castle, along with other children's favorites, dotted the grounds. She'd hired a company to provide costumed characters to wander among the guests, taking pictures with the kids. Most of the little girls wore tiaras or princess caps while boys wore pirate hats and crowns.

Some were in costume, mostly the girls, of course. Who wouldn't want to be a princess for a day? Wearing a long pink dress and tiara, Jessica, a princess herself, wandered from activity to activity, her eagle eye checking on every detail. Everything appeared to be running smoothly.

Many of her volunteers had eagerly agreed to wear a costume as well. The pirate booth was popular. She spotted men and women in bright orange vests, like the DM's at the club, making their rounds with clipboards in hand.

Everywhere she glanced, children ran wildly across the wide expanse of green lawn. Adults, most in casual dress, gathered in groups. Some were wealthy patrons they were hoping to convince to dig deep into their wallets for the auction that would take place in her father's ballroom tonight.

That had been another brilliant idea. A raffle offered during the picnic to encourage everyone to participate. She'd paired an adult with a child to wander and sell tickets. Most attendees would shell out five bucks for a ticket or buy more just to support the cause. And for those who wanted and needed something a bit more formal with a fair amount of pandering, the price of a dinner ticket got them an evening at her father's mansion with an auction following in the ballroom.

Other guests included community and business leaders who'd donated their time, money, goodies to be auctioned or raffled. Many had volunteered to help run the event. Like the mayor who'd been dunked twice in the last thirty minutes, once by the commissioner himself.

Yes, it was going quite well. Thank god. She pressed her fist into her stomach to calm the nervous fluttering.

Two little girls, ages four and six ran up to her. They'd been her shadow on and off for most of the day. It made her sad to realize they didn't have a real home or that the two girls, along with a younger child, were living apart.

Instead of finding stable foster homes, they'd been shifted from home to home. Their parents had died and with no other family, the trio were wards of the state. She remembered Jason and how it had hurt him to be separated from his sister because no one wanted two children. It wasn't right. She took their hands.

"You're a princess," Mara, the youngest said. Her blonde hair was in two cute ponytails with ribbons tied in bows to match her Cinderella dress.

Her sister Sarah rolled her eyes. "No she's not."

But her wistful sigh said she wished she believed in fairy tales and happy endings. She wore a dress with the characters from a popular children's movie on the bodice and a sparkling tiara in her hair. Jessica had shopped for the visiting children, choosing complete outfits for each child.

Smiling, Jessica asked, "Have you gotten yourselves a hot dog yet?"

When they said no, she grinned. "Come on. Let's eat. I'm starved."

She led the way to the big monstrosity her father called his new barbeque. The man himself operated the fire-breathing beast. At her approach, he lifted his brow. She shook her head. No renting a grill for Roland Lowe, and she had to admit, he looked relaxed in his backseat role at her event—well, the charities event. But it was her baby.

Her poor father had been flustered and outraged when she'd told him her plans. For the first time in her life, she hadn't asked her father for permission. He'd finally accepted her decision to work for Jasen…after a fashion.

"Looking good, princess," he said.

"See, I told you she's a princess," the younger girl whispered to her sister.

Her father glanced at the girls. "I believe there are three beautiful princesses standing before me, and I bet you all want a hot dog."

Mara jumped up and down, but Sarah scuffed her foot on the brand new stone patio.

Jessica knelt. "What do you want, Sarah?"

"I'd rather have a hamburger. My foster mom makes me a hot dog every time she fixes steak or hamburgers for everyone else. I don't like hot dogs so much anymore."

Her heart bled for this child. She'd heard enough horror stories of how foster children were often treated differently from birth children. It firmed her resolve to do what she could for as many displaced children as she could. Starting with these two. "Well, this is a magical place, Sarah, and you can have a hamburger. Or a sausage. Or even one of those skewers of beef."

The girl's eyes brightened, and after grabbing three plates, she took her young charges to a table where Mara bit into her hot dog eagerly and Jessica and Sarah pulled teriyaki soaked meat off charred, bamboo skewers.

****

Jasen stood on the covered patio with Glorie, Bryce, and Jaimie. Lucy and Graham wandered over to join them. All of them were staying for the late dinner even though Bryce and Graham had already made more than generous contributions. Tiny fairy-like lights blinked and twinkled under the shaded roofline and inside every pop-up tent. As he glanced around his friends, his heart swelled with pride.

The event was a success. The scents of cooking meat and the sounds of happy cries and screams and lots of laughter filled the air. Volunteers mingled with prospective foster parents who mingled with the movers and shakers of San Francisco and the surrounding community. The jump houses were full of energetic children, and the splash pad she'd put in was filled with shrieking kids of all ages. Supervising adults sat around in chairs. Each activity station was busy.

"Wonder where she got the idea for a fairy tale theme?" Bryce's eyes twinkled with humor.

"Well, she got her idea at your ball," Jasen admitted. "Insisted we go back." He sighed. He'd had such plans for that night, but the two of them had worked instead and he'd found working with Jessica both fascinating and nearly as exhilarating as an evening of sex.

"She looks good with those girls," Glorie said, a pleased gleam in her eyes.

"Yeah, she does. Their social worker brought them in the hopes of finding a permanent home for the three of them so they can remain together." Before damage from being in the system took hold.

"Three?"

He pointed to a matronly woman carting a crying toddler toward Jessica. Sarah rushed forward, took her baby sister, and carried her back to Jessica. Jessica accepted the child rather awkwardly, yet as she talked softly and jiggled, the baby slumped over and rested her blonde head against Jessica's shoulder.

Jasen's heart stopped. The sight of four blonde heads so closely together brought warmth seeping into his chest. They looked like a family. A mother and her daughters. Suddenly, it wasn't enough to just dream of living with his princess. He wanted to make her his queen and add a few princesses and maybe even a dark haired prince to the mix.

Pulling out his phone, he snapped a photo. For a moment, he felt lost and lonely as those long ago bad memories surfaced. Suddenly, he wanted Jessica, wanted to be near her and hear her voice, to catch the love for him that shone in her eyes.

"Excuse me," he said to his friends.

As he strode away, he heard Bryce congratulate Glorie on another successful match. He grinned. Yes, he had a lot to thank both Bryce and Glorie for. Had he not accepted their invitation to their latest event or gone with his gut and chosen Jessica, he'd never have gotten to know the real woman hidden deep within the spoiled rich girl exterior she presented to the world.

"Can a lowly servant join the party?" he asked as he approached his princess.

Jessica's bright smile chased the shadows of his past from his mind.

"You, Sir, are not a lowly servant. You are a prince."

"Well this prince is claiming his princess when the night is over. No more waiting."

Grinning, Jessica lowered her lashes demurely. "Yes, Sir." She turned to the children.

Mara's eyes were wide, her chin sporting a smear of ketchup. Taking a napkin, Jessica wiped her mouth. "Now, there are a lot of fun things happening out here. Sarah, take Mara to the princess castle for a little while."

"Are you going to leave?"

Jessica smiled gently. "No, sweetheart. I'll be here until the very end."

"Promise?"

"I double-triple promise." Both girls raced off. The social worker reached for the slumped child in Jessica's arms, but she shook her head. "She's good. Go ahead and get some food and relax for a while." Until becoming involved with Jasen, and visiting and meeting many of the families here today, she'd never in her life held a child. To have one fall asleep so trustingly touched her deeply.

"I'm proud of you, princess." He fingered the baby's curls.

She smiled, but her eyes were serious. "Does that mean I get the job?"

Caught up in the moment and his dreams, Jasen realized he'd forgotten that the position she'd grasped with both hands and took charge of, as she'd taken charge of his heart, was only temporary. He'd hired her to put on this one event. Guilt slid through his mind. She'd worked hard to prove, not just to him, that she was useful but to herself. He should have realized she'd have been fretting and stewing.

He lifted her hand and kissed her fingers. "The job has been yours since the night of the ball when you utterly amazed me. And turned my life upside down."

She breathed out a huge sigh of relief. "Thank you, Jasen."

He grinned. "Does this mean you'll date the boss now?"

She chuckled softly. "Yes, as long as my boss realizes he's dating a woman who's not afraid to go after what she wants." Jessica lifted one hand and grazed his cheek with the back of her fingertips. "And this woman wants this very bossy man who showed her she was worth more than just her good looks or her money. But before you go making plans, I have something I want to show you." She shifted the baby in her arms slightly and pulled a small square of paper from her pocket. "You once asked me what I had of value. I told you about my stuffed dog, but there is one other thing." She handed him her treasure.

Jasen unfolded the sheet of paper, and his brows rose as he scanned her final report card received in her senior year. Circled in red was the A she'd received in their lab class. She watched his expression, the way his eyes narrowed, the parting of his full lips, and the slight frown across his forehead. "You kept your report card?"

She smiled. "No, I kept the accomplishment and the reminder of the nerd who'd actually expected me to pull my weight. That A means the world to me."

"It's not your only A." In fact, the A's and B's impressed him.

She blinked back tears. "It's the only A I ever earned on my own. I didn't buy that A, Jasen, because this nerdy kid was pretty domineering and bossy and wouldn't cave. His life would have been easier, but he didn't take the easy way out or allow me to do the same." She pulled his head down. "Thank you."

He kissed her back, folded the sheet of paper, and handed it to her. "If we're playing show and tell, I have something for you." He slid his phone from his pocket and brought up the image of her. "No matter how many phones I've had, this picture of you has been with me. There was something haunting and sad about you, and I never forgot you."

Her eyes filled with tears as she stared at an old photo of herself. "What a pair we are."

"I love you, Jessica. I want more than just dinners and walks in the park. I want to wake up with you beside me and fall asleep with you in my arms. And I want everything in between for all time. Will you marry me? Be my princess forever?"

She smiled. "I'll still be rich and maybe sometimes, a bit spoiled."

He chuckled. "I wouldn't have you any other way, Jessica." He leaned close and kissed her. "Is that a yes?"

"What about a family?" She patted the stirring toddler's back.

"I want a family with you, but if you don't want one, I can accept that."

She grinned. "How do you feel about an instant family of say…three girls?"

Jasen felt the love in his heart swelling to near bursting. He held out his phone, swiped the screen a few times, and held it out, showing the photo of four blonde princesses, each of them smiling and laughing. "I think this would make me the happiest man on earth."

"Me, too. I want to marry you immediately. And I'm putting my foot down. No fancy wedding, no big social event. Just a quiet ceremony. The soon to be Mr. and Mrs. McPherson have a lot to do to get ready to make a home for their girls."

Sarah and Mara, on their way back to Jessica, spotted Jasen with his arm around Jessica. Sarah stopped short and grabbed Mara's arms. He held open his arms, inviting the girls to join them. Not just for a day. The nerdy kid turned Dom had his princess and a forever family of his own.

Epilogue

"Girls are with your father," Jasen announced as he hurried into the bedroom to change. "Are you ready to go?"

"You bet." Just waiting for you. Hurry up. The limo will be here any minute. She wore a short skirt, sans panties, and a low-cut blouse that revealed more than it hid. "You know my father's going to spoil them outrageously."

"They deserve it. He was so excited. Something about a pony." He made quick work of stripping and donning a new costume.

"Are you serious?" Jessica's jaw had dropped.

Grinning, he shook his head. "I'd say the barn I saw means he bought his granddaughters a pony. I'd say our daughters are in good hands." Dressed, he pulled her into his arms. "Are you nervous about the weekend?"

"Are you kidding? Pleasure Manor is well named. I can't believe we are going back. This is our third event. I talked to Jaimie, and she said she'll be there with Bryce, along with Lucy and Graham, and a bunch of new people."

"You can still change your mind about the show. No one would hold it against you."

"No way." Since the fairy tale event and her starring role on spanking, she and Jasen had given several demonstrations at the club, minus the fucking. That they saved and took to one of the rooms or to his office. Of course, with three girls, they didn't get a chance to get away often.

He nuzzled her neck. "I'm proud of you, princess. You could have said no."

She arched her brows. "Does anyone say no to Glorie?"

"Never. But be warned, it'll be intense."

"Anything involving Glorie is intense. Besides, we've done this before." And holy mother of god, four-way sex with the Domme and her partner was always amazingly good.

"Not in front of others."

After watching Goldie and her three partners and hearing the responses of those watching, Jessica's new fantasy was going to come true tomorrow night. "Let's move it, Master McPherson. I have places to go, people to see, and orgasms just waiting to happen."

"There you go again, giving orders, princess."

"Yeah, until we get into the back seat of the limo, we're just man and wife."

"Oh? What are we in the car?"

"A Dom and a very naughty sub who just might need spanking tonight."

About the Author

Sydney St. Claire is the pseudonym of Susan Edwards, author of Historical Native American/Western/Paranormal romances and of the popular White Series. During her career, she has been nominated for the Romantic Times Career Achievement Award for Western Historical and Reviewer's Choice Best Book Award.

Sydney takes her readers into the world of erotic romance where her characters come together in explosive passion as they solve life's problems and find true love along with the best sex our hero and heroine have ever experienced.

She credits her mother for her writing success. Encouraged to read, Susan always preferred happy endings, which meant romances were her favorite genre.

Susan resides in California. Her office is quite crowded with two small dogs at her feet, another huge girl in her recliner, and five cats to keep her company while she writes. Life gets fun when all five insist on supervising…

When not writing, she enjoys crafts including quilting, sewing, cross-stitch, and knitting. She and her husband of thirty-plus years are avid gardeners. Camping, fishing, biking, and hiking are other outdoor pursuits she enjoys. She is, of course, an avid reader and hates cooking and housework.

Contact Susan/Sydney at:
Facebook
https://www.facebook.com/sydneystclaire
Twitter
https://twitter.com/Sydneystclaire
Email
sydneystclaire@aol.com or
susan@susanedwards.com
Blog
http://sydneystclaire.com/blog
Goodreads
https://www.goodreads.com/sydneystclaire
http://sydneystclaire.com
http://susanedwards.com

To chat with Sydney and other Wild Rose Press
authors of erotic romance, join us at
www.groups.yahoo.com/group/thewilderroses.

Also Available

Beauty Submits to Her Beast
Once Upon a Dom Book 4
by Sydney St. Claire
https://amzn.com/B0105AFAZY

Rancher Caitlin Olsen is in complete control of her life. After years of taking care of others, she's on her own and loving every minute. She has her horses and her ranch. What more does she need? Yet deep inside, she yearns to give up all her responsibilities and simply experience life. When a friend suggests she try a bit of BDSM role-play, she does her research and accepts an invitation to Pleasure Manor for a fairy tale event.

Former Navy SEAL and Dominant, Damon Steele is a loner. His failure to keep his team alive destroyed too many hopes and dreams. He won't be responsible for anyone else's life or happiness ever again. There's no room in his life—or his heart—for romance. Instead, he satisfies his needs at BDSM clubs and never with the same sub. Taking part in the fairy tale event at Pleasure Manor is difficult enough, but when Beauty challenges him both in the bedroom and out, he's not sure he can control his inner beast.

Also Read

Kiltless in Carolina
by Ashantay Peters
https://amzn.com/B01BX04JWA

Unable to say no to family, photographer Isla McAllister agrees to attend the Highland Games under one condition—no roughing it. She wants a comfy hotel room where she can escape her family's matchmaking schemes and avoid her ex-fiancé? Her plans go awry when she discovers her room has been given to a hot highlander with a smile that resurrects forgotten fantasies. Unfortunately, he's a kilt-wearing piper, just like her ex.

After a bad breakup, Graeme MacKay plans on getting laid during the Games. He's gone too long with his bagpipes as the only instrument getting any play. His number one criteria for the woman who'll share his bed—she has to be a non-Scot. But when he clashes with a feisty MacAllister who claims he stole her room, he throws caution to the wind and offers to share his room…and his bed.

Thank you for purchasing this
publication of The Wild Rose Press, Inc.
If you enjoyed the story, we would appreciate
your letting others know by leaving a review.
For other wonderful stories, please visit our
on-line bookstore at www.wilderroses.com.

For questions or more
information contact us at
info@thewildrosepress.com.

The Wild Rose Press, Inc.
www.thewilderroses.com

Stay current with The Wild Rose Press, Inc.
Like us on Facebook
https://www.facebook.com/TheWildRosePress
And Follow us on Twitter
https://twitter.com/WildRosePress